# SAKI

## THE SECRET SIN OF SEPTIMUS BROPE AND OTHER STORIES

PENGU

## PENGUIN BOOKS

Published by the Penguin Group. Penguin Books Ltd, 27 Wrights Lane,
London w8 5tz, England. Penguin Books USA Inc., 375 Hudson Street,
New York, New York 10014, USA. Penguin Books Australia Ltd, Ringwood,
Victoria, Australia. Penguin Books Canada Ltd, 10 Alcorn Avenue, Toronto,
Ontario, Canada m4v 3b2. Penguin Books (NZ) Ltd, 182–190 Wairau Road,
Auckland 10, New Zealand · Penguin Books Ltd, Registered Offices: Har-
mondsworth, Middlesex, England · **These stories have been taken from**
*The Complete Saki*, **published by Penguin Books in 1982** · This edition
published 1995 · Typeset by Datix International Ltd, Bungay, Suffolk. Printed in
England by Clays Ltd, St Ives plc · Except in the United States of America, this
book is sold subject to the condition that it shall not, by way of trade or otherwise,
be lent, re-sold, hired out, or otherwise circulated without the publisher's prior
consent in any form of binding or cover other than that in which it is published
and without a similar condition including this condition being imposed on the
subsequent purchaser · 10 9 8 7 6 5 4 3 2 1

# CONTENTS

# Reginald

I did it – I should have known better. I persuaded Reginald to go to the McKillops' garden-party against his will.

We all make mistakes occasionally. 'They know you're here, and they'll think it so funny if you don't go. And I want particularly to be in with Mrs McKillop just now.'

'I know, you want one of her smoke Persian kittens as a prospective wife for Wumples – or a husband, is it?' (Reginald has a magnificent scorn for details, other than sartorial.) 'And I am expected to undergo social martyrdom to suit the connubial exigencies –'

'Reginald! It's nothing of the kind, only I'm sure Mrs McKillop would be pleased if I brought you. Young men of your brilliant attractions are rather at a premium at her garden-parties.'

'Should be at a premium in heaven,' remarked Reginald complacently.

'There will be very few of you there, if that is what you mean. But seriously, there won't be any great strain upon your powers of endurance; I promise you that you shan't have to play croquet, or talk to the Archdeacon's wife, or do anything that is likely to bring on physical prostration. You can just wear your sweetest clothes and a moderately amiable expression, and eat chocolate-creams with the appetite of a *blasé* parrot. Nothing more is demanded of you.'

Reginald shut his eyes. 'There will be the exhaustingly up-to-date young women who will ask me if I have seen *San Toy*; a less progressive grade who will yearn to hear about the Diamond Jubilee – the historic event, not the horse. With a little encouragement, they will inquire if I saw the Allies march into Paris. Why are women so fond of raking up the past? They're as bad as tailors, who invariably remember what you owe them for a suit long after you've ceased to wear it.'

'I'll order lunch for one o'clock; that will give you two and a half hours to dress in.'

Reginald puckered his brow into a tortured frown, and I knew that my point was gained. He was debating what tie would go with which waistcoat.

Even then I had my misgivings.

During the drive to the McKillops' Reginald was possessed with a great peace, which was not wholly to be accounted for by the fact that he had inveigled his feet into shoes a size too small for them. I misgave more than ever, and having once launched Reginald on to the McKillops' lawn, I established him near a seductive dish of *marrons glacés*, and as far from the Archdeacon's wife as possible; as I drifted away to a diplomatic distance I heard with painful distinctness the eldest Mawkby girl asking him if he had seen *San Toy*.

It must have been ten minutes later, not more, and I had been having *quite* an enjoyable chat with my hostess, and had promised to lend her *The Eternal City* and my recipe for rabbit mayonnaise, and was just about to offer a kind home for her third Persian kitten, when I perceived, out of the corner of my eye, that Reginald was not where I had left him, and that the *marrons glacés* were untasted. At the same moment I became aware that old Colonel Mendoza was essaying to tell his classic story of how he introduced golf into India, and that Reginald was in dangerous proximity. There are occasions when Reginald is caviare to the Colonel.

'When I was at Poona in '76 –'

'My dear Colonel,' purred Reginald, 'fancy admitting such a thing! Such a give-away for one's age! I wouldn't admit being on this planet in '76.' (Reginald in his wildest lapses into veracity never admits to being more than twenty-two.)

The Colonel went to the colour of a fig that has attained great ripeness, and Reginald, ignoring my efforts to intercept him, glided away to another part of the lawn. I found him a few minutes later happily engaged in teaching the youngest Rampage boy the approved theory of mixing absinthe, within full earshot of his mother. Mrs Rampage occupies a prominent place in local Temperance movements.

As soon as I had broken up this unpromising *tête-à-tête* and settled Reginald where he could watch the croquet players losing their tempers, I wandered off to find my hostess and renew the kitten negotiations at the point where they had been interrupted. I did not succeed in running her down at once, and eventually it was Mrs McKillop who sought me out, and her conversation was not of kittens.

'Your cousin is discussing *Zaza* with the Archdeacon's wife; at least, he is discussing, she is ordering her carriage.'

She spoke in the dry, staccato tone of one who repeats a French exercise, and I knew that as far as Millie McKillop was concerned, Wumples was devoted to a lifelong celibacy.

'If you don't mind,' I said hurriedly, 'I think we'd like our carriage ordered too,' and I made a forced march in the direction of the croquet ground.

I found every one talking nervously and feverishly of the weather and the war in South Africa, except Reginald, who was 3 reclining in a comfortable chair with the dreamy, far-away look that a volcano might wear just after it had desolated entire villages. The Archdeacon's wife was buttoning up her gloves with a concentrated deliberation that was fearful to behold. I shall have to treble my subscription to her Cheerful Sunday Evenings Fund before I dare set foot in her house again.

At that particular moment the croquet players finished their game, which had been going on without a symptom of finality during the whole afternoon. Why, I ask, should it have stopped precisely when a counter-attraction was so necessary? Every one seemed to drift towards the area of disturbance, of which the chairs of the Archdeacon's wife and Reginald formed the storm-centre. Conversation flagged, and there settled upon the company that expectant hush that precedes the dawn – when your neighbours don't happen to keep poultry.

'What did the Caspian Sea?' asked Reginald, with appalling suddenness.

There were symptoms of a stampede. The Archdeacon's wife looked at me. Kipling or some one has described somewhere the look a foundered camel gives when the caravan moves on and leaves it to its fate. The peptonized reproach in the good lady's eyes brought the passage vividly to my mind.

I played my last card.

'Reginald, it's getting late, and a sea-mist is coming on.' I knew that the elaborate curl over his right eyebrow was not guaranteed to survive a sea-mist.

'Never, never again, will I take you to a garden-party. Never . . . You behaved abominably . . . What did the Caspian see?'

A shade of genuine regret for misused opportunities passed over Reginald's face.

'After all,' he said, 'I believe an apricot tie would have gone better with the lilac waistcoat.'

# Reginald on the Academy

'One goes to the Academy in self-defence,' said Reginald. 'It is the one topic one has in common with the Country Cousins.'

'It is almost a religious observance with them,' said the Other. 'A kind of artistic Mecca, and when the good ones die they go –'

'To the Chantrey Bequest. The mystery is *what* they find to talk about in the country.'

'There are two subjects of conversation in the country: servants, and can fowls be made to pay? The first, I believe, is compulsory, the second optional.'

'As a function,' resumed Reginald, 'the Academy is a failure.'

'You think it would be tolerable without the pictures?'

'The pictures are all right, in their way; after all, one can always *look* at them if one is bored with one's surroundings, or wants to avoid an imminent acquaintance.'

'Even that doesn't always save one. There is the inevitable female whom you met once in Devonshire, or the Matoppo Hills, or somewhere, who charges up to you with the remark that it's funny how one always meets people one knows at the Academy. Personally, I *don't* think it funny.'

'I suffered in that way just now,' said Reginald plaintively, 'from a woman whose word I had to take that she had met me last summer in Brittany.'

'I hope you were not too brutal?'

'I merely told her with engaging simplicity that the art of life was the avoidance of the unattainable.'

6  'Did she try and work it out on the back of her catalogue?'

'Not there and then. She murmured something about being "so clever". Fancy coming to the Academy to be clever!'

'To be clever in the afternoon argues that one is dining nowhere in the evening.'

'Which reminds me that I can't remember whether I accepted an invitation from you to dine at Kettner's tonight.'

'On the other hand, I can remember with startling distinctness not having asked you to.'

'So much certainty is unbecoming in the young; so we'll consider that settled. What were you talking about? Oh, pictures. Personally, I rather like them; they are so refreshingly real and probable, they take one away from the unrealities of life.'

'One likes to escape from oneself occasionally.'

'That is the disadvantage of a portrait; as a rule, one's bitterest friends can find nothing more to ask than the faithful unlikeness that goes down to posterity as oneself. I hate posterity – it's so fond of having the last word. Of course, as regards portraits, there are exceptions.'

'For instance?'

'To die before being painted by Sargent is to go to heaven prematurely.'

'With the necessary care and impatience, you may avoid that catastrophe.'

'If you're going to be rude,' said Reginald, 'I shall dine with you tomorrow night as well. The chief vice of the Academy,' he continued, 'is its nomenclature. Why, for instance, should an obvious trout-stream with a palpable rabbit sitting in the foreground be called "an evening dream of unbeclouded peace", or something of that sort?'

'You think,' said the Other, 'that a name should economize description rather than stimulate imagination?'

'Properly chosen, it should do both. There is my lady kitten at home, for instance; I've called it Derry.'

'Suggests nothing to my imagination but protracted sieges and religious animosities. Of course, I don't know your kitten –'

'Oh, you're silly. It's a sweet name, and it answers to it – when it wants to. Then, if there are any unseemly noises in the night, they can be explained succinctly: Derry and Toms.'

'You might almost charge for the advertisement. But as applied to pictures, don't you think your system would be too subtle, say, for the Country Cousins?'

'Every reformation must have its victims. You can't expect the fatted calf to share the enthusiasm of the angels over the prodigal's return. Another darling weakness of the Academy is that none of its luminaries must "arrive" in a hurry. You can see them coming for years, like a Balkan trouble or a street improvement, and by the time they have painted a thousand or so square yards of canvas, their work begins to be recognized.'

'Someone who Must Not be Contradicted said that a man must be a success by the time he's thirty, or never.'

'To have reached thirty,' said Reginald, 'is to have failed in life.'

# Reginald at the Theatre

'After all,' said the Duchess vaguely, 'there are certain things you can't get away from. Right and wrong, good conduct and moral rectitude, have certain well-defined limits.'

'So, for the matter of that,' replied Reginald, 'has the Russian Empire. The trouble is that the limits are not always in the same place.'

Reginald and the Duchess regarded each other with mutual distrust, tempered by a scientific interest. Reginald considered that the Duchess had much to learn; in particular, not to hurry out of the Carlton as though afraid of losing one's last bus. A woman, he said, who is careless of disappearances is capable of leaving town before Goodwood, and dying at the wrong moment of an unfashionable disease.

The Duchess thought that Reginald did not exceed the ethical standard which circumstances demanded.

'Of course,' she resumed combatively, 'it's the prevailing fashion to believe in perpetual change and mutability, and all that sort of thing, and to say we are all merely an improved form of primeval ape – of course you subscribe to that doctrine?'

'I think it decidedly premature; in most people I know the process is far from complete.'

'And equally of course you are quite irreligious?'

'Oh, by no means. The fashion just now is a Roman Catholic frame of mind with an Agnostic conscience: you get the mediaeval picturesqueness of the one with the modern conveniences of the other.'

The Duchess suppressed a sniff. She was one of those people who regard the Church of England with patronizing affection, as if it were something that had grown up in their kitchen garden.

'But there are other things,' she continued, 'which I suppose are to a certain extent sacred even to you. Patriotism, for instance, and Empire, and Imperial responsibility, and blood-is-thicker-than-water, and all that sort of thing.'

Reginald waited for a couple of minutes before replying, while the Lord of Rimini temporarily monopolized the acoustic possibilities of the theatre.

'That is the worst of a tragedy,' he observed, 'one can't always hear oneself talk. Of course I accept the Imperial idea and the responsibility. After all, I would just as soon think in Continents as anywhere else. And some day, when the season is over and we have the time, you shall explain to me the exact blood-brotherhood and all that sort of thing that exists between a French Canadian and a mild Hindoo and a Yorkshireman, for instance.'

'Oh, well, "dominion over palm and pine", you know,' quoted the Duchess hopefully; 'of course we mustn't forget that we're all part of the great Anglo-Saxon Empire.'

'Which for its part is rapidly becoming a suburb of Jerusalem. A very pleasant suburb, I admit, and quite a charming Jerusalem. But still a suburb.'

'Really, to be told one's living in a suburb when one is conscious of spreading the benefits of civilization all over the world! Philanthropy – I suppose you will say *that* is a comfortable delusion; and yet even you must admit that whenever want or misery or starvation is known to exist, however distant or difficult of access, we instantly organize relief on the most generous scale, and distribute it, if need be, to the uttermost ends of the earth.'

The Duchess paused, with a sense of ultimate triumph. She had made the same observation at a drawing-room meeting, and it had been extremely well received.

'I wonder,' said Reginald, 'if you have ever walked down the Embankment on a winter night?'

'Gracious, no, child! Why do you ask?'

'I didn't; I only wondered. And even your philanthropy, practised in a world where everything is based on competition, must have a debit as well as a credit account. The young ravens cry for food.'

'And are fed.'

'Exactly. Which presupposes that something else is fed upon.'

'Oh, you're simply exasperating. You've been reading Nietzsche till you haven't got any sense of moral proportion left. May I ask if you are governed by *any* laws of conduct whatever?'

'There are certain fixed rules that one observes for one's own comfort. For instance, never be flippantly rude to any inoffensive grey-bearded stranger that you may meet in pine forests or hotel smoking-rooms on the Continent. It always turns out to be the King of Sweden.'

'The restraint must be dreadfully irksome to you. When I was younger, boys of your age used to be nice and innocent.'

'Now we are only nice. One must specialize in these days. Which reminds me of the man I read of in some sacred book who was given a choice of what he most desired. And because he didn't ask for titles and honours and dignities, but only for immense wealth, these other things came to him also.'

'I am sure you didn't read about him in any sacred book.'

'Yes; I fancy you will find him in Debrett.'

# Reginald on Worries

I have (said Reginald) an aunt who worries. She's not really an aunt – a sort of amateur one, and they aren't really worries. She is a social success, and has no domestic tragedies worth speaking of, so she adopts any decorative sorrows that are going, myself included. In that way she's the antithesis, or whatever you call it, to those sweet, uncomplaining women one knows who have seen trouble, and worn blinkers ever since. Of course, one just loves them for it, but I must confess they make me uncomfy; they remind one so of a duck that goes flapping about with forced cheerfulness long after its head's been cut off. Ducks have *no* repose. Now, my aunt has a shade of hair that suits her, and a cook who quarrels with the other servants, which is always a hopeful sign, and a conscience that's absentee for about eleven months of the year, and only turns up at Lent to annoy her husband's people, who are considerably Lower than the angels, so to speak: with all these natural advantages – she says her particular tint of bronze is a natural advantage, and there can be no two opinions as to the advantage – of course she has to send out for her afflictions, like those restaurants where they haven't got a licence. The system has this advantage, that you can fit your unhappiness in with your other engagements, whereas real worries have a way of arriving at meal-times, and when you're dressing, or other solemn moments. I knew a canary once that had been trying for months and years to hatch out a family, and every one looked upon it as a blameless infatuation, like the sale of Delagoa Bay, which would be an annual loss to the Press agencies if it ever came to pass; and one day the bird really did bring it off, in the middle of family prayers. I say the middle, but it was also the end: you can't go on being thankful for daily bread when you are wondering what on earth very new canaries expect to be fed on.

At present she's rather in a Balkan state of mind about the treatment of the Jews in Roumania. Personally, I think the Jews have estimable qualities; they're so kind to their poor – and to our rich. I daresay in Roumania the cost of living beyond one's income isn't so great. Over here the trouble is that so many people who have money to throw about seem to have such vague ideas where to throw it. That fund, for instance, to relieve the victims of sudden disasters – what is a sudden disaster? There's Marion Mulciber, who *would* think she could play bridge, just as she would think she could ride down a hill on a bicycle; on that occasion she went to a hospital, now she's gone into a Sisterhood – lost all she had, you know, and gave the rest to Heaven. Still, you can't call it a sudden calamity; *that* occurred when poor dear Marion was born. The doctors said at the time that she couldn't live more than a fortnight, and she's been trying ever since to see if she could. Women are so opinionated.

And then there's the Education Question – not that I can see that there's anything to worry about in that direction. To my mind, education is an absurdly overrated affair. At least, one never took it very seriously at school, where everything was done to bring it prominently under one's notice. Anything that is worth knowing one practically teaches oneself, and the rest obtrudes itself sooner or later. The reason one's elders know so comparatively little is because they have to unlearn so much that they acquired by way of education before we were born. Of course I'm a believer in Nature-study; as I said to Lady Beauwhistle, if you want a lesson in elaborate artificiality, just watch the studied unconcern of a Persian cat entering a crowded salon, and then go and practise it for a fortnight. The Beauwhistles weren't born in the Purple, you know, but they're getting there on the instalment system – so much down, and the rest when you feel like it. They have kind hearts, and they never forget birthdays. I forget what he was, something in the City, where the patriotism comes from; and she – oh, well, her frocks are built in Paris, but she wears them with a strong English accent. So public-spirited of her. I think she must have been very strictly brought up, she's so desperately anxious to do the wrong thing correctly. Not that it really matters nowadays, as I told her: I know some perfectly virtuous people who are received everywhere.

# The Innocence of Reginald

Reginald slid a carnation of the newest shade into the buttonhole of his latest lounge coat, and surveyed the result with approval. 'I am just in the mood,' he observed, 'to have my portrait painted by some one with an unmistakable future. So comforting to go down to posterity as *Youth with a Pink Carnation* in catalogue-company with *Child with Bunch of Primroses*, and all that crowd.'

'Youth,' said the Other, 'should suggest innocence.'

'But never act on the suggestion. I don't believe the two ever really go together. People talk vaguely about the innocence of a little child, but they take mighty good care not to let it out of their sight for twenty minutes. The watched pot never boils over. I knew a boy once who really was innocent; his parents were in Society, but they never gave him a moment's anxiety from his infancy. He believed in company prospectuses, and in the purity of elections, and in women marrying for love, and even in a system for winning at roulette. He never quite lost his faith in it, but he dropped more money than his employers could afford to lose. When last I heard of him, he was believing in his innocence; the jury weren't. All the same, I really am innocent just now of something every one accuses me of having done, and so far as I can see, their accusations will remain unfounded.'

'Rather an unexpected attitude for you.'

'I love people who do unexpected things. Didn't you always adore the man who slew a lion in a pit on a snowy day? But about this unfortunate innocence. Well, quite long ago, when I'd been quarrelling with more people than usual, you among the number – it must have been in November, I never quarrel with you too near Christmas – I had an idea that I'd like to write a book. It was to be a book of personal reminiscences, and was to leave out nothing.'

'Reginald!'

'Exactly what the Duchess said when I mentioned it to her. I was provoking and said nothing, and the next thing, of course, was that every one heard that I'd written the book and got it in the press. After that, I might have been a goldfish in a glass bowl for all the privacy I got. People attacked me about it in the most unexpected places, and implored or commanded me to leave out things that I'd forgotten had ever happened. I sat behind Miriam Klopstock one night in the dress-circle at His Majesty's, and she began at once about the incident of the Chow dog in the bathroom, which she insisted must be struck out. We had to argue it in a disjointed fashion, because some of the people wanted to listen to the play, and Miriam takes nines in voices. They had to stop her playing in the "Macaws" Hockey Club because you could hear what she thought when her shins got mixed up in a scrimmage for half a mile on a still day. They are called the Macaws because of their blue-and-yellow costumes, but I understand there was nothing yellow about Miriam's language. I agreed to make one alteration, as I pretended I had got it a Spitz instead of a Chow, but beyond that I was firm. She megaphoned back two minutes later, "You promised you would never mention it; don't you ever keep a promise?" When people had stopped glaring in our direction, I replied that I'd as soon think of keeping white mice. I saw her tearing little bits out of her programme for a minute or two, and then she leaned back and snorted, "You're not the boy I took you for," as though she were an eagle arriving at Olympus with the wrong Ganymede. That was her last audible remark, but she went on tearing up her programme and scattering the pieces around her, till one of her neighbours asked with immense dignity whether she should send for a wastepaper-basket. I didn't stay for the last act.

'Then there is Mrs – oh, I never can remember her name; she lives in a street that the cabmen have never heard of, and is at home on Wednesdays. She frightened me horribly once at a private view by saying mysteriously, "I oughtn't to be here, you know; this is one of my days." I thought she meant that she was subject to periodical outbreaks and was expecting an attack at any moment. So embarrassing if she had suddenly taken it into her head that she was Cesare Borgia or St Elizabeth of Hungary. That sort of thing would make one unpleasantly conspicuous even at a private view. However, she merely meant to say that it was Wednesday, which at the moment was incontrovertible. Well, she's on quite a different tack to the Klopstock. She doesn't visit anywhere very extensively, and, of course, she's awfully keen for me to drag in an incident that occurred at one of the Beauwhistle garden-parties, when she says she accidentally hit the shins of a Serene Somebody or other with a croquet mallet and that he swore at her in German. As a matter of fact, he went on discoursing on the Gordon-Bennett affair in French. (I never can remember if it's a new submarine or a divorce. Of course, how stupid of me!) To be disagreeably exact, I fancy she missed him by about two inches – over-anxiousness, probably – but she likes to think she hit him. I've felt that way with a partridge which I always imagine keeps on flying strong, out of false pride, till it's the other side of the hedge. She said she could tell me everything she was wearing on the occasion. I said I didn't want my book to read like a laundry list, but she explained that she didn't mean those sort of things.

'And there's the Chilworth boy, who can be charming as long as he's content to be stupid and wear what he's told to; but he gets the idea now and then that he'd like to be epigrammatic, and the result is like watching a rook trying to build a nest in a gale. Since he got wind of the book, he's been persecuting me to work in something of his about the Russians and the Yalu Peril, and is quite sulky because I won't do it.

'Altogether, I think it would be rather a brilliant inspiration if you were to suggest a fortnight in Paris.'

# The Baker's Dozen

### Characters

MAJOR RICHARD DUMBARTON
MRS CAREWE
MRS PALY–PAGET

*Scene: deck of eastward-bound steamer. Major Dumbarton seated on deck-chair, another chair by his side, with the name 'Mrs Carewe' painted on it, a third near by. Enter, R., Mrs Carewe, seats herself leisurely in her deck-chair, the Major affecting to ignore her presence.*

MAJOR: (*Turning suddenly*) Emily! After all these years! This is fate!

EM.: Fate! Nothing of the sort; it's only me. You men are always such fatalists. I deferred my departure three whole weeks, in order to come out in the same boat that I saw you were travelling by. I bribed the steward to put our chairs side by side in an unfrequented corner, and I took enormous pains to be looking particularly attractive this morning, and then you say, 'This is fate.' I *am* looking particularly attractive, am I not?

MAJ.: More than ever. Time has only added a ripeness to your charms.

EM.: I knew you'd put it exactly in those words. The phraseology of love-making is awfully limited, isn't it? After all, the chief charm is in the fact of being made love to. You *are* making love to me, aren't you?

MAJ.: Emily dearest, I had already begun making advances, even before you sat down here. I also bribed the steward to put our seats together in a secluded corner. 'You may consider it done, sir,' was his reply. That was immediately after breakfast.

EM.: How like a man to have his breakfast first. I attended to the seat business as soon as I left my cabin.

MAJ.: Don't be unreasonable. It was only at breakfast that I discovered your blessed presence on the boat. I paid violent and unusual attention to a flapper all through the meal in order to make you jealous. She's probably in her cabin writing reams about me to a fellow-flapper at this very moment.

EM.: You needn't have taken all that trouble to make me jealous, Dickie. You did that years ago, when you married another woman.

MAJ.: Well, you had gone and married another man – a widower, too, at that.

EM.: Well, there's no particular harm in marrying a widower, I suppose. I'm ready to do it again, if I meet a really nice one.

MAJ.: Look here, Emily, it's not fair to go at that rate. You're a lap ahead of me the whole time. It's my place to propose to you; all you've got to do is to say 'yes'.

EM.: Well, I've practially said it already, so we needn't dawdle over that part.

MAJ.: Oh, well –
(*They look at each other, then suddenly embrace with considerable energy.*)

MAJ.: We dead-heated it that time. (*Suddenly jumping to his feet*) Oh, d – I'd forgotten!

EM.: Forgotten what?

MAJ.: The children. I ought to have told you. Do you mind children?

EM.: Not in moderate quantities. How many have you got?

MAJ.: (*counting hurriedly on his fingers*) Five.

EM.: Five!

MAJ.: (*Anxiously*) Is that too many?

EM.: It's rather a number. The worst of it is, I've some myself.

MAJ.: Many?

EM.: Eight.

MAJ.: Eight in six years! Oh, Emily!

EM.: Only four were my own. The other four were by my husband's first marriage. Still, that practically makes eight.

MAJ.: And eight and five make thirteen. We can't start our married life with thirteen children; it would be most unlucky. (*Walks up and down in agitation*) Some way must be found out of this. If we could only bring them down to twelve. Thirteen is so horribly unlucky.

EM.: Isn't there some way by which we could part with one or two? Don't the French want more children? I've often seen articles about it in the *Figaro*.

MAJ.: I fancy they want French children. Mine don't even speak French.

EM.: There's always a chance that one of them might turn out depraved and vicious, and then you could disown him. I've heard of that being done.

MAJ.: But, good gracious, you've got to educate him first. You can't expect a boy to be vicious till he's been to a good school.

EM.: Why couldn't he be naturally depraved? Lots of boys are.

MAJ.: Only when they inherit it from depraved parents. You don't suppose there's any depravity in me, do you?

EM.: It sometimes skips a generation, you know. Weren't any of your family bad?

21

MAJ.: There was an aunt who was never spoken of.

EM.: There you are!

MAJ.: But one can't build too much on that. In mid-Victorian days they labelled all sorts of things as unspeakable that we should speak about quite tolerantly. I daresay this particular aunt had only married a Unitarian, or rode to hounds on both sides of her horse, or something of that sort. Anyhow, we can't wait indefinitely for one of the children to take after a doubtfully depraved great aunt. Something else must be thought of.

EM.: Don't people ever adopt children from other families?

MAJ.: I've heard of it being done by childless couples, and those sort of people –

EM.: Hush! Some one's coming. Who is it?

MAJ.: Mrs Paly-Paget.

EM.: The very person!

MAJ.: What, to adopt a child? Hasn't she got any?

EM.: Only one miserable hen-baby.

MAJ.: Let's sound her on the subject.

(*Enter Mrs Paly-Paget, R.*)

Ah, good morning, Mrs Paly-Paget. I was just wondering at breakfast where did we meet last?

MRS P.-P.: At the Criterion, wasn't it? (*Drops into vacant chair*)

MAJ.: At the Criterion, of course.

MRS P.-P.: I was dining with Lord and Lady Slugford. Charming people, but so mean. They took us afterwards to the Velo-drome, to see some dancer interpreting Mendelssohn's 'songs without clothes'. We were all packed up in a little box near the roof, and you may imagine how hot it was. It was like a Turkish bath. And, of course, one couldn't see anything.

MAJ.: Then it was not like a Turkish bath.

MRS P.-P.: Major!

EM.: We were just talking of you when you joined us.

MRS P.-P.: Really! Nothing very dreadful, I hope.

EM.: Oh, dear, no! It's too early on the voyage for that sort of thing. We were feeling rather sorry for you.

MRS P.-P.: Sorry for me? Whatever for?

MAJ.: Your childless hearth and all that, you know. No little pattering feet.

MRS P.-P.: Major! How dare you? I've got my little girl, I suppose you know. Her feet can patter as well as other children's.

MAJ.: Only one pair of feet.

MRS P.-P.: Certainly. My child isn't a centipede. Consdering the way they move us about in those horrid jungle stations, without a decent bungalow to set one's foot in, I consider I've got a heartless child, rather than a childless hearth. Thank you for your sympathy all the same. I daresay it was well meant. Impertinence often is.

EM.: Dear Mrs Paly-Paget, we were only feeling sorry for your sweet little girl when she grows older, you know. No little brothers and sisters to play with.

MRS P.-P.: Mrs Carewe, this conversation strikes me as being indelicate, to say the least of it. I've only been married two and a half years, and my family is naturally a small one.

MAJ.: Isn't it rather an exaggeration to talk of one little female child as a family? A family suggests numbers.

MRS P.-P.: Really, Major, your language is extraordinary. I daresay I've only got a little female child, as you call it, at present –

MAJ.: Oh, it won't change into a boy later on, if that's what you're counting on. Take our word for it; we've had so much    23 more experience in these affairs than you have. Once a female, always a female. Nature is not infallible, but she always abides by her mistakes.

MRS P.-P.: (*Rising*) Major Dumbarton, these boats are uncomfortably small, but I trust we shall find ample accommodation for avoiding each other's society during the rest of the voyage. The same wish applies to you, Mrs Carewe.

(*Exit Mrs Paly-Paget, L.*)

MAJ.: What an unnatural mother! (*Sinks into chair*)

EM.: I wouldn't trust a child with any one who had a temper like hers. Oh, Dickie, why did you go and have such a large family? You always said you wanted me to be the mother of your children.

MAJ.: I wasn't going to wait while you were founding and fostering dynasties in other directions. Why you couldn't be content to have children of your own, without collecting them like batches of postage stamps, I can't think. The idea of marrying a man with four children!

EM.: Well, you're asking me to marry one with five.

MAJ.: Five! (*Springing to his feet*) Did I say five?

EM.: You certainly said five.

MAJ.: Oh, Emily, supposing I've miscounted them! Listen now, keep count with me. Richard – that's after me, of course.

EM.: One.

MAJ.: Albert-Victor – that must have been in Coronation year.

EM.: Two!

MAJ.: Maud. She's called after –

EM.: Never mind who she's called after. Three!

MAJ.: And Gerald.

24  EM.: Four!

MAJ.: That's the lot.

EM.: Are you sure?

MAJ.: I swear that's the lot. I must have counted Albert-Victor as two.

EM.: Richard!

MAJ.: Emily!

(*They embrace.*)

# The Mouse

Theodoric Voler had been brought up, from infancy to the confines of middle age, by a fond mother whose chief solicitude had been to keep him screened from what she called the coarser realities of life. When she died she left Theodoric alone in a world that was as real as ever, and a good deal coarser than he considered it had any need to be. To a man of his temperament and upbringing even a simple railway journey was crammed with petty annoyances and minor discords, and as he settled himself down in a second-class compartment one September morning he was conscious of ruffled feelings and general mental discomposure. He had been staying at a country vicarage, the inmates of which had been certainly neither brutal nor bacchanalian, but their supervision of the domestic establishment had been of that lax order which invites disaster. The pony carriage that was to take him to the station had never been properly ordered, and when the moment for his departure drew near the handyman who should have produced the required article was nowhere to be found. In this emergency Theodoric, to his mute but very intense disgust, found himself obliged to collaborate with the vicar's daughter in the task of harnessing the pony, which necessitated groping about in an ill-lighted outhouse called a stable, and smelling very like one – except in patches where it smelt of mice. Without being actually afraid of mice, Theodoric classed them among the coarser incidents of life, and considered that Providence, with a little exercise of moral courage, might long ago have recognized that they were not indispensable, and

26

have withdrawn them from circulation. As the train glided out of the station Theodoric's nervous imagination accused himself of exhaling a weak odour of stableyard, and possibly of displaying a mouldy straw or two on his usually well-brushed garments. Fortunately the only other occupant of the compartment, a lady of about the same age as himself, seemed inclined for slumber rather than scrutiny; the train was not due to stop till the terminus was reached, in about an hour's time, and the carriage was of the old-fashioned sort, that held no communication with a corridor, therefore no further travelling companions were likely to intrude on Theodoric's semi-privacy. And yet the train had scarcely attained its normal speed before he became reluctantly but vividly aware that he was not alone with the slumbering lady; he was not even alone in his own clothes. A warm, creeping movement over his flesh betrayed the unwelcome and highly resented presence, unseen but poignant, of a strayed mouse, that had evidently dashed into its present retreat during the episode of the pony harnessing. Furtive stamps and shakes and wildly directed pinches failed to dislodge the intruder, whose motto, indeed, seemed to be Excelsior; and the lawful occupant of the clothes lay back against the cushions and endeavoured rapidly to evolve some means for putting an end to the dual ownership. It was unthinkable that he should continue for the space of a whole hour in the horrible position of a Rowton House for vagrant mice (already his imagination had at least doubled the numbers of the alien invasion). On the other hand, nothing less drastic than partial disrobing would ease him of his tormentor, and to undress in the presence of a lady, even for so laudable a purpose, was an idea that made his eartips tingle in a blush of abject shame. He had never been able to bring himself even to the mild exposure of open-work socks in the presence of the fair sex. And yet – the lady in this case was to all appearances soundly and securely asleep; the mouse, on the other hand, seemed to be trying to crowd a Wanderjahr into a few strenuous minutes. If there is any truth in the theory of transmigration, this particular mouse must certainly have been in a former state a member of the Alpine Club. Sometimes in its eagerness it lost its footing and slipped for half an inch or so; and then, in fright, or more probably temper, it bit. Theodoric was goaded into the most audacious undertaking of his life. Crimsoning to the hue of a beetroot and keeping an agonized watch on his slumbering fellow-traveller, he swiftly and noiselessly secured the ends of his railway-rug to the racks on either side of the carriage, so that a substantial curtain hung athwart the compartment. In the narrow dressing-room that he had thus improvised he proceeded with violent haste to extricate himself partially and the mouse entirely from the surrounding casings of tweed and half-wool. As the unravelled mouse gave a wild leap to the floor, the rug, slipping its fastening at either end, also came down with a heart-curdling flop, and almost simultaneously the awakened sleeper opened her eyes. With a movement almost quicker than the mouse's, Theodoric pounced on the rug, and hauled its ample folds chin-high over his dismantled person as he collapsed into the further corner of the carriage. The blood raced and beat in the veins of his neck and forehead, while he waited dumbly for the communication-cord to be pulled. The lady, however, contented herself with a silent stare at her strangely muffled companion. How much had she seen, Theodoric queried to himself, and in any case what on earth must she think of his present posture?

'I think I have caught a chill,' he ventured desperately.

'Really, I'm sorry,' she replied. 'I was just going to ask you if you would open this window.'

'I fancy it's malaria,' he added, his teeth chattering slightly, as much from fright as from a desire to support his theory.

'I've got some brandy in my hold-all, if you'll kindly reach it down for me,' said his companion.

'Not for worlds – I mean, I never take anything for it,' he assured her earnestly.

'I suppose you caught it in the Tropics?'

Theodoric, whose acquaintance with the Tropics was limited to an annual present of a chest of tea from an uncle in Ceylon, felt that even the malaria was slipping from him. Would it be possible, he wondered, to disclose the real state of affairs to her in small instalments?

'Are you afraid of mice?' he ventured, growing, if possible, more scarlet in the face.

'Not unless they came in quantities, like those that ate up Bishop Hatto. Why do you ask?'

'I had one crawling inside my clothes just now,' said Theodoric in a voice that hardly seemed his own. 'It was a most awkward situation.'

'It must have been, if you wear your clothes at all tight,' she observed; 'but mice have strange ideas of comfort.'

'I had to get rid of it while you were asleep,' he continued; then, with a gulp, he added, 'it was getting rid of it that brought me to – to this.'

'Surely leaving off one small mouse wouldn't bring on a chill,' she exclaimed, with a levity that Theodoric accounted abominable.

Evidently she had detected something of his predicament, and was enjoying his confusion. All the blood in his body seemed to have mobilized in one concentrated blush, and an agony of abasement, worse than a myriad mice, crept up and down over his soul. And then, as reflection began to assert itself, sheer terror took the place of humiliation. With every minute that passed the train was rushing nearer to the crowded and bustling terminus where dozens of prying eyes would be exchanged for the one paralysing pair that watched him from the further corner of the carriage. There was one slender despairing chance, which the next few minutes must decide. His fellow-traveller might relapse into a blessed slumber. But as the minutes throbbed by that chance ebbed away. The furtive glance which Theodoric stole at her from time to time disclosed only an unwinking wakefulness.

'I think we must be getting near now,' she presently observed.

Theodoric had already noted with growing terror the recurring stacks of small, ugly dwellings that heralded the journey's end. The words acted as a signal. Like a hunted beast breaking cover and dashing madly towards some other haven of momentary safety he threw aside his rug, and struggled frantically into his dishevelled garments. He was conscious of dull suburban stations racing past the window, of a choking, hammering sensation in his throat and heart, and of an icy silence in that corner towards which he dared not look. Then as he sank back in his seat, clothed and almost delirious, the train slowed down to a final crawl, and the woman spoke.

'Would you be so kind,' she asked, 'as to get me a porter to put me into a cab? It's a shame to trouble you when you're feeling unwell, but being blind makes one so helpless at a railway station.'

# Tobermory

It was a chill, rain-washed afternoon of a late August day, that indefinite season when partridges are still in security or cold storage, and there is nothing to hunt – unless one is bounded on the north by the Bristol Channel, in which case one may lawfully gallop after fat red stags. Lady Blemley's house-party was not bounded on the north by the Bristol Channel, hence there was a full gathering of her guests round the tea-table on this particular afternoon. And, in spite of the blankness of the season and the triteness of the occasion, there was no trace in the company of that fatigued restlessness which means a dread of the pianola and a subdued hankering for auction bridge. The undisguised open-mouthed attention of the entire party was fixed on the homely negative personality of Mr Cornelius Appin. Of all her guests, he was the one who had come to Lady Blemley with the vaguest reputation. Some one had said he was 'clever', and he had got his invitation in the moderate expectation, on the part of his hostess, that some portion at least of his cleverness would be contributed to the general entertainment. Until tea-time that day she had been unable to discover in what direction, if any, his cleverness lay. He was neither a wit nor a croquet champion, a hypnotic force nor a begetter of amateur theatricals. Neither did his exterior suggest the sort of man in whom women are willing to pardon a generous measure of mental deficiency. He had subsided into mere Mr Appin, and the Cornelius seemed a piece of transparent baptismal bluff. And now he was claiming to have launched on the world a discovery beside which the invention of gunpowder, of the printing-press, and of steam locomotion were inconsiderable trifles. Science had made bewildering strides in many directions during recent decades, but this thing seemed to belong to the domain of miracle rather than to scientific achievement.

'And do you really ask us to believe,' Sir Wilfrid was saying, 'that you have discovered a means for instructing animals in the art of human speech, and that dear old Tobermory has proved your first successful pupil?'

'It is a problem at which I have worked for the last seventeen years,' said Mr Appin, 'but only during the last eight or nine months have I been rewarded with glimmerings of success. Of course I have experimented with thousands of animals, but latterly only with cats, those wonderful creatures which have assimilated themselves so marvellously with our civilization while retaining all their highly developed feral instincts. Here and there among cats one comes across an outstanding superior intellect, just as one does among the ruck of human beings, and when I made the acquaintance of Tobermory a week ago I saw at once that I was in contact with a "Beyond-cat" of extra-ordinary intelligence. I had gone far along the road to success in recent experiments; with Tobermory, as you call him, I have reached the goal.'

Mr Appin concluded his remarkable statement in a voice which he strove to divest of a triumphant inflection. No one said, 'Rats,' though Clovis's lips moved in a monosyllabic contortion which probably invoked those rodents of disbelief.

'And do you mean to say,' asked Miss Resker, after a slight pause, 'that you have taught Tobermory to say and understand easy sentences of one syllable?'

'My dear Miss Resker,' said the wonder-worker patiently,

'one teaches little children and savages and backward adults in that piecemeal fashion; when one has once solved the problem of making a beginning with an animal of highly developed intelligence one has no need for those halting methods. Tobermory can speak our language with perfect correctness.'

This time Clovis very distinctly said, 'Beyond-rats!' Sir Wilfrid was more polite, but equally sceptical.

'Hadn't we better have the cat in and judge for ourselves?' suggested Lady Blemley.

Sir Wilfrid went in search of the animal, and the company settled themselves down to the languid expectation of witnessing some more or less adroit drawing-room ventriloquism.

In a minute Sir Wilfrid was back in the room, his face white beneath its tan and his eyes dilated with excitement.

'By Gad, it's true!'

His agitation was unmistakably genuine, and his hearers started forward in a thrill of awakened interest.

Collapsing into an armchair he continued breathlessly: 'I found him dozing in the smoking-room and called out to him to come for his tea. He blinked at me in his usual way, and I said, "Come on, Toby; don't keep us waiting"; and, by Gad! he drawled out in a most horribly natural voice that he'd come when he dashed well pleased! I nearly jumped out of my skin!'

Appin had preached to absolutely incredulous hearers; Sir Wilfrid's statement carried instant conviction. A Babel-like chorus of startled exclamation arose, amid which the scientist sat mutely enjoying the first fruit of his stupendous discovery.

In the midst of the clamour Tobermory entered the room and made his way with velvet tread and studied unconcern across to the group seated round the tea-table.

A sudden hush of awkwardness and constraint fell on the

company. Somehow there seemed an element of embarrassment in addressing on equal terms a domestic cat of acknowledged dental ability.

'Will you have some milk, Tobermory?' asked Lady Blemley in a rather strained voice.

'I don't mind if I do,' was the response, couched in a tone of even indifference. A shiver of suppressed excitement went through the listeners, and Lady Blemley might be excused for pouring out the saucerful of milk rather unsteadily.

'I'm afraid I've spilt a good deal of it,' she said apologetically.

'After all, it's not my Axminster,' was Tobermory's rejoinder.

Another silence fell on the group, and then Miss Resker, in her best district-visitor manner, asked if the human language had been difficult to learn. Tobermory looked squarely at her for a moment and then fixed his gaze serenely on the middle distance. It was obvious that boring questions lay outside his scheme of life.

'What do you think of human intelligence?' asked Mavis Pellington lamely.

'Of whose intelligence in particular?' asked Tobermory coldly.

'Oh, well, mine for instance,' said Mavis, with a feeble laugh.

'You put me in an embarrassing position,' said Tobermory, whose tone and attitude certainly did not suggest a shred of embarrassment. 'When your inclusion in this house-party was suggested Sir Wilfrid protested that you were the most brainless woman of his acquaintance, and that there was a wide distinction between hospitality and the care of the feeble-minded. Lady Blemley replied that your lack of brain-power was the precise quality which had earned you your invitation, as you were the only person she could think of who might be idiotic enough to buy their old car. You know, the one they call "The Envy of Sisyphus", because it goes quite nicely up-hill if you push it.'

Lady Blemley's protestations would have had greater effect if she had not casually suggested to Mavis only that morning that the car in question would be just the thing for her down at her Devonshire home.

Major Barfield plunged in heavily to effect a diversion.

'How about your carryings-on with the tortoise-shell puss up at the stables, eh?'

The moment he had said it every one realized the blunder.

'One does not usually discuss these matters in public,' said Tobermory frigidly. 'From a slight observation of your ways since you've been in this house I should imagine you'd find it inconvenient if I were to shift the conversation on to your own little affairs.'

The panic which ensued was not confined to the Major.

'Would you like to go and see if cook has got your dinner ready?' suggested Lady Blemley hurriedly, affecting to ignore the fact that it wanted at least two hours to Tobermory's dinner-time.

'Thanks,' said Tobermory, 'not quite so soon after my tea. I don't want to die of indigestion.'

'Cats have nine lives, you know,' said Sir Wilfred heartily.

'Possibly,' answered Tobermory, 'but only one liver.'

'Adelaide!' said Mrs Cornett, 'do you mean to encourage that cat to go out and gossip about us in the servants' hall?'

The panic had indeed become general. A narrow ornamental balustrade ran in front of most of the bedroom windows at the Towers, and it was recalled with dismay that this had formed a favourite promenade for Tobermory at all hours, whence he could watch the pigeons – and heaven knew what else besides. If he intended to become reminiscent in his present outspoken strain the effect would be something more than disconcerting.

Mrs Cornett, who spent much time at her toilet table, and whose complexion was reputed to be of a nomadic though punctual disposition, looked as ill at ease as the Major. Miss Scrawen, who wrote fiercely sensuous poetry and led a blameless life, merely displayed irritation; if you are methodical and virtuous in private you don't necessarily want every one to know it. Bertie van Tahn, who was so depraved at seventeen that he had long ago given up trying to be any worse, turned a dull shade of gardenia white, but he did not commit the error of dashing out of the room like Odo Finsberry, a young gentleman who was understood to be reading for the Church and who was possibly disturbed at the thought of scandals he might hear concerning other people. Clovis had the presence of mind to maintain a composed exterior; privately he was calculating how long it would take to procure a box of fancy mice through the agency of the *Exchange and Mart* as a species of hush-money.

Even in a delicate situation like the present, Agnes Resker could not endure to remain too long in the background.

'Why did I ever come down here?' she asked dramatically.

Tobermory immediately accepted the opening.

'Judging by what you said to Mrs Cornett on the croquet-lawn yesterday, you were out for food. You described the Blemleys as the dullest people to stay with that you knew, but said they were clever enough to employ a first-rate cook; otherwise they'd find it difficult to get any one to come down a second time.'

'There's not a word of truth in it! I appeal to Mrs Cornett –' exclaimed the discomfited Agnes.

'Mrs Cornett repeated your remark afterwards to Bertie van Tahn,' continued Tobermory, 'and said, "That woman is a regular Hunger Marcher; she'd go anywhere for four square meals a day," and Bertie van Tahn said –'

At this point the chronicle mercifully ceased. Tobermory had caught a glimpse of the big yellow Tom from the Rectory working his way through the shrubbery towards the stable wing. In a flash he had vanished through the open French window.

With the disappearance of his too brilliant pupil Cornelius Appin found himself beset by a hurricane of bitter upbraiding, anxious inquiry, and frightened entreaty. The responsibility for the situation lay with him, and he must prevent matters from becoming worse. Could Tobermory impart his dangerous gift to other cats? was the first question he had to answer. It was possible, he replied, that he might have initiated his intimate friend the stable puss into his new accomplishment, but it was unlikely that his teaching could have taken a wider range as yet.

'Then,' said Mrs Cornett, 'Tobermory may be a valuable cat and a great pet; but I'm sure you'll agree, Adelaide, that both he and the stable cat must be done away with without delay.'

'You don't suppose I've enjoyed the last quarter of an hour, do you?' said Lady Blemley bitterly. 'My husband and I are very fond of Tobermory – at least, we were before this horrible accomplishment was infused into him; but now, of course, the only thing is to have him destroyed as soon as possible.'

'We can put some strychnine in the scraps he always gets at dinner-time,' said Sir Wilfrid, 'and I will go and drown the stable cat myself. The coachman will be very sore at losing his pet, but I'll say a very catching form of mange has broken out in both cats and we're afraid of its spreading to the kennels.'

'But my great discovery!' expostulated Mr Appin; 'after all my years of research and experiment –'

'You can go and experiment on the short-horns at the farm, who are under proper control,' said Mrs Cornett, 'or the elephants at the Zoological Gardens. They're said to be highly intelligent, and they have this recommendation, that they don't come creeping about our bedrooms and under chairs, and so forth.'

An archangel ecstatically proclaiming the Millennium, and then finding that it clashed unpardonably with Henley and would have to be indefinitely postponed, could hardly have felt more crestfallen than Cornelius Appin at the reception of his wonderful achievement. Public opinion, however, was against him – in fact, had the general voice been consulted on the subject it is probable that a strong minority vote would have been in favour of including him in the strychnine diet.

Defective train arrangements and a nervous desire to see matters brought to a finish prevented an immediate dispersal of the party, but dinner that evening was not a social success. Sir Wilfrid had had rather a trying time with the stable cat and subsequently with the coachman. Agnes Resker ostentatiously limited her repast to a morsel of dry toast, which she bit as though it were a personal enemy; while Mavis Pellington maintained a vindictive silence throughout the meal. Lady Blemley kept up a flow of what she hoped was conversation, but her attention was fixed on the doorway. A plateful of carefully dosed fish scraps was in readiness on the sideboard, but sweets and savoury and dessert went their way, and no Tobermory appeared either in the dining-room or kitchen.

The sepulchral dinner was cheerful compared with the subsequent vigil in the smoking-room. Eating and drinking had at least supplied a distraction and cloak to the prevailing embarrassment. Bridge was out of the question in the general tension of nerves and tempers, and after Odo Finsberry had given a lugubrious rendering of 'Mélisande in the Wood' to a frigid audience, music was tacitly avoided. At eleven the servants went to bed, announcing that the small window in the pantry had been left open as usual for Tobermory's private use. The guests read steadily through the current batch of magazines, and fell back gradually on the 'Badminton Library' and bound volumes of *Punch*. Lady Blemley made periodic visits to the pantry, returning each time with an expression of listless depression which forestalled questioning.

At two o'clock Clovis broke the dominating silence.

'He won't turn up tonight. He's probably in the local newspaper office at the present moment, dictating the first instalment of his reminiscences. Lady What's-her-name's book won't be in it. It will be the event of the day.'

Having made this contribution to the general cheerfulness, Clovis went to bed. At long intervals the various members of the house-party followed his example.

The servants taking round the early tea made a uniform announcement in reply to a uniform question. Tobermory had not returned.

Breakfast was, if anything, a more unpleasant function than dinner had been, but before its conclusion the situation was relieved. Tobermory's corpse was brought in from the shrubbery, where a gardener had just discovered it. From the bites on his throat and the yellow fur which coated his claws it was evident that he had fallen in unequal combat with the big Tom from the Rectory.

By midday most of the guests had quitted the Towers, and after lunch Lady Blemley had sufficiently recovered her spirits to write an extremely nasty letter to the Rectory about the loss of her valuable pet.

Tobermory had been Appin's one successful pupil, and he was destined to have no successor. A few weeks later an elephant    39 in the Dresden Zoological Garden, which had shown no previous signs of irritability, broke loose and killed an Englishman who had apparently been teasing it. The victim's name was variously reported in the papers as Oppin and Eppelin, but his front name was faithfully rendered Cornelius.

'If he was trying German irregular verbs on the poor beast,' said Clovis, 'he deserved all he got.'

# The Secret Sin of Septimus Brope

'Who and what is Mr Brope?' demanded the aunt of Clovis suddenly.

Mrs Riversedge, who had been snipping off the heads of defunct roses, and thinking of nothing in particular, sprang hurriedly to mental attention. She was one of those old-fashioned hostesses who consider that one ought to know something about one's guests, and that the something ought to be to their credit.

'I believe he comes from Leighton Buzzard,' she observed by way of preliminary explanation.

'In these days of rapid and convenient travel,' said Clovis, who was dispersing a colony of green-fly with visitations of cigarette smoke, 'to come from Leighton Buzzard does not necessarily denote any great strength of character. It might only mean a mere restlessness. Now if he had left it under a cloud, or as a protest against the incurable and heartless frivolity of its inhabitants, that would tell us something about the man and his mission in life.'

'What does he do?' pursued Mrs Troyle magisterially.

'He edits the *Cathedral Monthly*,' said her hostess, 'and he's enormously learned about memorial brasses and transepts and the influence of Byzantine worship on modern liturgy, and all those sort of things. Perhaps he is just a little bit heavy and immersed in one range of subjects, but it takes all sorts to make a good house-party, you know. You don't find him *too* dull, do you?'

'Dullness I could overlook,' said the aunt of Clovis: 'what I cannot forgive is his making love to my maid.'

'My dear Mrs Troyle,' gasped the hostess, 'what an extraordinary idea! I assure you Mr Brope would not dream of doing such a thing.'

'His dreams are a matter of indifference to me; for all I care his slumbers may be one long indiscretion of unsuitable erotic advances, in which the entire servants' hall may be involved. But in his waking hours he shall not make love to my maid. It's no use arguing about it, I'm firm on the point.'

'But you must be mistaken,' persisted Mrs Riversedge; 'Mr Brope would be the last person to do such a thing.'

'He is the first person to do such a thing, as far as my information goes, and if I have any voice in the matter he certainly shall be the last. Of course, I am not referring to respectably intentioned lovers.'

'I simply cannot think that a man who writes so charmingly and informingly about transepts and Byzantine influences would behave in such an unprincipled manner,' said Mrs Riversedge; 'what evidence have you that he's doing anything of the sort? I don't want to doubt your word, of course, but we mustn't be too ready to condemn him unheard, must we?'

'Whether we condemn him or not, he has certainly not been unheard. He has the room next to my dressing-room, and on two occasions, when I dare say he thought I was absent, I have plainly heard him announcing through the wall, "I love you, Florrie." Those partition walls upstairs are very thin; one can almost hear a watch ticking in the next room.'

'Is your maid called Florence?'

'Her name is Florinda.'

'What an extraordinary name to give a maid!'

'I did not give it to her; she arrived in my service already christened.'

'What I mean is,' said Mrs Riversedge, 'that when I get maids with unsuitable names I call them Jane; they soon get used to it.'

'An excellent plan,' said the aunt of Clovis coldly; 'unfortunately I have got used to being called Jane myself. It happens to be my name.'

She cut short Mrs Riversedge's flood of apologies by abruptly remarking:

'The question is not whether I'm to call my maid Florinda, but whether Mr Brope is to be permitted to call her Florrie. I am strongly of opinion that he shall not.'

'He may have been repeating the words of some song,' said Mrs Riversedge hopefully; 'there are lots of those sorts of silly refrains with girls' names,' she continued, turning to Clovis as a possible authority on the subject. '"You mustn't call me Mary –"'

'I shouldn't think of doing so,' Clovis assured her; 'in the first place, I've always understood that your name was Henrietta; and then I hardly know you well enough to take such a liberty.'

'I mean there's a *song* with that refrain,' hurriedly explained Mrs Riversedge, 'and there's "Rhoda, Rhoda kept a pagoda", and "Maisie is a daisy", and heaps of others. Certainly it doesn't sound like Mr Brope to be singing such songs, but I think we ought to give him the benefit of the doubt.'

'I had already done so,' said Mrs Troyle, 'until further evidence came my way.'

She shut her lips with the resolute finality of one who enjoys the blessed certainty of being implored to open them again.

'Further evidence!' exclaimed her hostess; 'do tell me!'

'As I was coming upstairs after breakfast Mr Brope was just 43 passing my room. In the most natural way in the world a piece of paper dropped out of a packet that he held in his hand and fluttered to the ground just at my door. I was going to call out to him, "You've dropped something," and then for some reason I held back and didn't show myself till he was safely in his room. You see, it occurred to me that I was very seldom in my room just at that hour, and that Florinda was almost always there tidying up things about that time. So I picked up that innocent-looking piece of paper.'

Mrs Troyle paused again, with the self-applauding air of one who has detected an asp lurking in an apple charlotte.

Mrs Riversedge snipped vigorously at the nearest rose bush, incidentally decapitating a Viscountess Folkestone that was just coming into bloom.

'What was on the paper?' she asked.

'Just the words, in pencil, "I love you, Florrie" and then underneath, crossed out with a faint line, but perfectly plain to read, "Meet me in the garden by the yew."'

'There *is* a yew tree at the bottom of the garden,' admitted Mrs Riversedge.

'At any rate he appears to be truthful,' commented Clovis.

'To think that a scandal of this sort should be going on under my roof!' said Mrs Riversedge indignantly.

'I wonder why it is that scandal seems so much worse under a roof,' observed Clovis; 'I've always regarded it as a proof of the superior delicacy of the cat tribe that it conducts most of its scandals above the slates.'

'Now I come to think of it,' resumed Mrs Riversedge, 'there are things about Mr Brope that I've never been able to account for. His income, for instance: he only gets two hundred a year as editor of the *Cathedral Monthly*, and I know that his people are quite poor, and he hasn't any private means. Yet he manages to afford a flat somewhere in Westminster, and he goes abroad to Bruges and those sorts of places every year, and always dresses well, and gives quite nice luncheon-parties in the season. You can't do all that on two hundred a year, can you?'

'Does he write for any other papers?' queried Mrs Troyle.

'No, you see he specializes so entirely on liturgy and ecclesiastical architecture that his field is rather restricted. He once tried the *Sporting and Dramatic* with an article on church edifices in famous fox-hunting centres, but it wasn't considered of sufficient general interest to be accepted. No, I don't see how he can support himself in his present style merely by what he writes.'

'Perhaps he sells spurious transepts to American enthusiasts,' suggested Clovis.

'How could you sell a transept?' said Mrs Riversedge; 'such a thing would be impossible.'

'Whatever he may do to eke out his income,' interrupted Mrs Troyle, 'he is certainly not going to fill in his leisure moments by making love to my maid.'

'Of course not,' agreed her hostess; 'that must be put a stop to at once. But I don't quite know what we ought to do.'

'You might put a barbed wire entanglement round the yew tree as a precautionary measure,' said Clovis.

'I don't think that the disagreeable situation that has arisen is improved by flippancy,' said Mrs Riversedge; 'a good maid is a treasure –'

'I am sure I don't know what I should do without Florinda,' admitted Mrs Troyle; 'she understands my hair. I've long ago given up trying to do anything with it myself. I regard one's hair as I regard husbands: as long as one is seen together in public one's private divergences don't matter. Surely that was the luncheon gong.'

Septimus Brope and Clovis had the smoking-room to themselves after lunch. The former seemed restless and preoccupied, the latter quietly observant.

'What is a lorry?' asked Septimus suddenly; 'I don't mean the thing on wheels, of course I know what that is, but isn't there a bird with a name like that, the larger form of a lorikeet?'

'I fancy it's a lory, with one "r",' said Clovis lazily, 'in which case it's no good to you.'

Septimus Brope stared in some astonishment.

'How do you mean, no good to me?' he asked, with more than a trace of uneasiness in his voice.

'Won't rhyme with Florrie,' explained Clovis briefly.

Septimus sat upright in his chair, with unmistakable alarm on his face.

'How did you find out? I mean how did you know I was trying to get a rhyme to Florrie?' he asked sharply.

'I didn't know,' said Clovis, 'I only guessed. When you wanted to turn the prosaic lorry of commerce into a feathered poem flitting through the verdure of a tropical forest, I knew you must be working up a sonnet, and Florrie was the only female name that suggested itself as rhyming with lorry.'

Septimus still looked uneasy.

'I believe you know more,' he said.

Clovis laughed quietly, but said nothing.

'How much do you know?' Septimus asked desperately.

'The yew tree in the garden,' said Clovis.

'There! I felt certain I'd dropped it somewhere. But you must have guessed something before. Look here, you have surprised my secret. You won't give me away, will you? It is nothing to be ashamed of, but it wouldn't do for the editor of the *Cathedral* 46 *Monthly* to go in openly for that sort of thing, would it?'

'Well, I suppose not,' admitted Clovis.

'You see,' continued Septimus, 'I get quite a decent lot of money out of it. I could never live in the style I do on what I get as editor of the *Cathedral Monthly.*'

Clovis was even more startled than Septimus had been earlier in the conversation, but he was better skilled in repressing surprise.

'Do you mean to say you get money out of – Florrie?' he asked.

'Not out of Florrie, as yet,' said Septimus; 'in fact, I don't mind saying that I'm having a good deal of trouble over Florrie. But there are a lot of others.'

Clovis's cigarette went out.

'This is *very* interesting,' he said slowly. And then, with Septimus Brope's next words, illumination dawned on him.

'There are heaps of others; for instance:

> Cora with the lips of coral,
> You and I will never quarrel.

That was one of my earliest successes, and it still brings me in royalties. And then there is – "Esmeralda, when I first beheld her", and "Fair Teresa, how I love to please her", both of those have been fairly popular. And there is one rather dreadful one,' continued Septimus, flushing deep carmine, 'which has brought me in more money than any of the others:

> Lively little Lucie
> With her naughty nez retroussé

Of course, I loathe the whole lot of them; in fact, I'm rapidly becoming something of a woman-hater under their influence, but I can't afford to disregard the financial aspect of the matter. 47

And at the same time you can understand that my position as an authority on ecclesiastical architecture and liturgical subjects would be weakened, if not altogether ruined, if it once got about that I was the author of "Cora with the lips of coral" and all the rest of them.'

Clovis had recovered sufficiently to ask in a sympathetic, if rather unsteady, voice what was the special trouble with 'Florrie'.

'I can't get her into lyric shape, try as I will,' said Septimus mournfully. 'You see, one has to work in a lot of sentimental, sugary compliment with a catchy rhyme, and a certain amount of personal biography or prophecy. They've all of them got to have a long string of past successes recorded about them, or else you've got to foretell blissful things about them and yourself in the future. For instance, there is:

> Dainty little girlie Mavis,
> She is such a *rara avis*.
> All the money I can save is
> All to be for Mavis mine.

It goes to a sickening namby-pamby waltz tune, and for months nothing else was sung and hummed in Blackpool and other popular centres.'

This time Clovis's self-control broke down badly.

'Please excuse me,' he gurgled, 'but I can't help it when I remember the awful solemnity of that article of yours that you so kindly read us last night, on the Coptic Church in its relation to early Christian worship.'

Septimus groaned.

'You see how it would be,' he said; 'as soon as people knew me to be the author of that miserable sentimental twaddle, all respect for the serious labours of my life would be gone. I dare say I know more about memorial brasses than any one living, in fact I hope one day to publish a monograph on the subject, but I should be pointed out everywhere as the man whose ditties were in the mouths of nigger minstrels along the entire coast-line of our Island home. Can you wonder that I positively hate Florrie all the time that I'm trying to grind out sugar-coated rhapsodies about her?'

'Why not give free play to your emotions, and be brutally abusive? An uncomplimentary refrain would have an instant success as a novelty if you were sufficiently outspoken.'

'I never thought of that,' said Septimus, 'and I'm afraid I couldn't break away from the habit of fulsome adulation and suddenly change my style.'

'You needn't change your style in the least,' said Clovis; 'merely reverse the sentiment and keep to the inane phraseology of the thing. If you'll do the body of the song I'll knock off the refrain, which is the thing that principally matters, I believe. I shall charge half-shares in the royalties, and throw in my silence as to your guilty secret. In the eyes of the world you shall still be the man who has devoted his life to the study of transepts and Byzantine ritual; only sometimes, in the long winter evenings, when the wind howls drearily down the chimney and the rain beats against the windows, I shall think of you as the author of "Cora with the lips of coral". Of course, if in sheer gratitude at my silence you like to take me for a much needed holiday to the Adriatic or somewhere equally interesting, paying all expenses, I shouldn't dream of refusing.'

Later in the afternoon Clovis found his aunt and Mrs River-sedge indulging in gentle exercise in the Jacobean garden.

'I've spoken to Mr Brope about F.,' he announced.

'How splendid of you! What did he say?' came in a quick chorus from the two ladies.

'He was quite frank and straightforward with me when he saw that I knew his secret,' said Clovis, 'and it seems that his intentions were quite serious, if slightly unsuitable. I tried to show him the impracticability of the course that he was following. He said he wanted to be understood, and he seemed to think that Florinda would excel in that requirement, but I pointed out that there were probably dozens of delicately nurtured, pure-hearted young English girls who would be capable of understanding him, while Florinda was the only person in the world who understood my aunt's hair. That rather weighed with him, for he's not really a selfish animal, if you take him in the right way, and when I appealed to the memory of his happy childish days, spent amid the daisied fields of Leighton Buzzard (I suppose daisies do grow there), he was obviously affected. Anyhow, he gave me his word that he would put Florinda absolutely out of his mind, and he has agreed to go for a short trip abroad as the best distraction for his thoughts. I am going with him as far as Ragusa. If my aunt should wish to give me a really nice scarf-pin (to be chosen by myself), as a small recognition of the very considerable service I have done her, I shouldn't dream of refusing. I'm not one of those who think that because one is abroad one can go about dressed anyhow.'

A few weeks later in Blackpool and places where they sing, the following refrain held undisputed sway:

> How you bore me, Florrie,
> With those eyes of vacant blue;
> You'll be very sorry, Florrie,
> If I marry you.

Though I'm easy-goin', Florrie,
This I swear is true,
I'll throw you down a quarry, Florrie,
If I marry you.'

# The Hen

'Dora Bittholz is coming on Thursday,' said Mrs Sangrail.

'This next Thursday?' asked Clovis.

His mother nodded.

'You've rather done it, haven't you?' he chuckled. 'Jane Martlet has only been here five days, and she never stays less than a fortnight, even when she's asked definitely for a week. You'll never get her out of the house by Thursday.'

'Why should I?' asked Mrs Sangrail. 'She and Dora are good friends, aren't they? They used to be, as far as I remember.'

'They used to be; that's what makes them all the more bitter now. Each feels that she has nursed a viper in her bosom. Nothing fans the flame of human resentment so much as the discovery that one's bosom has been utilized as a snake sanatorium.'

'But what has happened? Has some one been making mischief?'

'Not exactly,' said Clovis; 'a hen came between them.'

'A hen? What hen?'

'It was a bronze Leghorn or some such exotic breed, and Dora sold it to Jane at a rather exotic price. They both go in for prize poultry, you know, and Jane thought she was going to get her money back in a large family of pedigree chickens. The bird turned out to be an abstainer from the egg habit, and I'm told that the letters which passed between the two women were a revelation as to how much invective could be got on to a sheet of notepaper.'

'How ridiculous!' said Mrs Sangrail. 'Couldn't some of their friends compose the quarrel?'

'People tried,' said Clovis, 'but it must have been rather like composing the storm music of the "Fliegende Holländer". Jane was willing to take back some of her most libellous remarks if Dora would take back the hen, but Dora said that would be owning herself in the wrong, and you know she'd as soon think of owning slum property in Whitechapel as do that.'

'It's a most awkward situation,' said Mrs Sangrail. 'Do you suppose they won't speak to one another?'

'On the contrary, the difficulty will be to get them to leave off. Their remarks on each other's conduct and character have hitherto been governed by the fact that only four ounces of plain speaking can be sent through the post for a penny.'

'I can't put Dora off,' said Mrs Sangrail. 'I've already postponed her visit once, and nothing short of a miracle would make Jane leave before her self-allotted fortnight is over.'

'Miracles are rather in my line,' said Clovis. 'I don't pretend to be very hopeful in this case, but I'll do my best.'

'As long as you don't drag me into it –' stipulated his mother.

'Servants are a bit of a nuisance,' muttered Clovis, as he sat in the smoking-room after lunch, talking fitfully to Jane Martlet in the intervals of putting together the materials of a cocktail, which he had irreverently patented under the name of an Ella Wheeler Wilcox. It was partly compounded of old brandy and partly of curaçao; there were other ingredients, but they were never indiscriminately revealed.

'Servants a nuisance!' exclaimed Jane, bounding into the topic with the exuberant plunge of a hunter when it leaves the high road and feels turf under its hoofs; 'I should think they were!

The trouble I've had in getting suited this year you would hardly believe. But I don't see what you have to complain of – your mother is so wonderfully lucky in her servants. Sturridge, for instance – he's been with you for years, and I'm sure he's a paragon as butlers go.'

'That's just the trouble,' said Clovis. 'It's when servants have been with you for years that they become a really serious nuisance. The "here today and gone tomorrow" sort don't matter – you've simply got to replace them; it's the stayers and the paragons that are the real worry.'

'But if they give satisfaction –'

'That doesn't prevent them from giving trouble. Now, you've mentioned Sturridge – it was Sturridge I was particularly thinking of when I made the observation about servants being a nuisance.'

'The excellent Sturridge a nuisance! I can't believe it.'

'I know he's excellent, and we just couldn't get along without him; he's the one reliable element in this rather haphazard household. But his very orderliness has had an effect on him. Have you ever considered what it must be like to go on unceasingly doing the correct thing in the correct manner in the same surroundings for the greater part of a lifetime? To know and ordain and superintend exactly what silver and glass and table linen shall be used and set out on what occasions, to have cellar and pantry and plate-cupboard under a minutely devised and undeviating administration, to be noiseless, impalpable, omnipresent, and, as far as your own department is concerned, omniscient?'

'I should go mad,' said Jane with conviction.

'Exactly,' said Clovis thoughtfully, swallowing his completed

54   Ella Wheeler Wilcox.

'But Sturridge hasn't gone mad,' said Jane with a flutter of inquiry in her voice.

'On most points he's thoroughly sane and reliable,' said Clovis, 'but at times he is subject to the most obstinate delusions, and on those occasions he becomes not merely a nuisance but a decided embarrassment.'

'What sort of delusions?'

'Unfortunately they usually centre round one of the guests of the house party, and that is where the awkwardness comes in. For instance, he took it into his head that Matilda Sheringham was the Prophet Elijah, and as all that he remembered about Elijah's history was the episode of the ravens in the wilderness he absolutely declined to interfere with what he imagined to be Matilda's private catering arrangements, wouldn't allow any tea to be sent up to her in the morning, and if he was waiting at table he passed her over altogether in handing round the dishes.'

'How very unpleasant. Whatever did you do about it?'

'Oh, Matilda got fed, after a fashion, but it was judged to be best for her to cut her visit short. It was really the only thing to be done,' said Clovis with some emphasis.

'I shouldn't have done that,' said Jane, 'I should have humoured him in some way. I certainly shouldn't have gone away.'

Clovis frowned.

'It is not always wise to humour people when they get these ideas into their heads. There's no knowing to what lengths they may go if you encourage them.'

'You don't mean to say he might be dangerous, do you?' asked Jane with some anxiety.

'One can never be certain,' said Clovis; 'now and then he gets some idea about a guest which *might* take an unfortunate turn. That is precisely what is worrying me at the present moment.'

'What, has he taken a fancy about some one here now?' asked Jane excitedly. 'How thrilling! Do tell me who it is.'

'You,' said Clovis briefly.

'Me?'

Clovis nodded.

'Who on earth does he think I am?'

'Queen Anne,' was the unexpected answer.

'Queen Anne! What an idea. But, anyhow, there's nothing dangerous about her; she's such a colourless personality.'

'What does posterity chiefly say about Queen Anne?' asked Clovis rather sternly.

'The only thing that I can remember about her,' said Jane, 'is the saying "Queen Anne's dead".'

'Exactly,' said Clovis, staring at the glass that had held the Ella Wheeler Wilcox, 'dead.'

'Do you mean he takes me for the ghost of Queen Anne?' asked Jane.

'Ghost? Dear, no. No one ever heard of a ghost that came down to breakfast and ate kidneys and toast and honey with a healthy appetite. No, it's the fact of you being so very much alive and flourishing that perplexes and annoys him. All his life he has been accustomed to look on Queen Anne as the personification of everything that is dead and done with, "as dead as Queen Anne", you know; and now he has to fill your glass at lunch and dinner and listen to your accounts of the gay time you had at the Dublin Horse Show, and naturally he feels that something's very wrong with you.'

'But he wouldn't be downright hostile to me on that account, would he?' Jane asked anxiously.

'I didn't get really alarmed about it till lunch today,' said Clovis; 'I caught him glowering at you with a very sinister look and muttering: "Ought to be dead long ago, she ought, and some one should see to it." That's why I mentioned the matter to you.'

'This is awful,' said Jane; 'your mother must be told about it at once.'

'My mother mustn't hear a word about it,' said Clovis earnestly; 'it would upset her dreadfully. She relies on Sturridge for everything.'

'But he might kill me at any moment,' protested Jane.

'Not at any moment; he's busy with the silver all the afternoon.'

'You'll have to keep a sharp look-out all the time and be on your guard to frustrate any murderous attack,' said Jane, adding in a tone of weak obstinacy: 'It's a dreadful situation to be in, with a mad butler dangling over you like the sword of What's-his-name, but I'm certainly not going to cut my visit short.'

Clovis swore horribly under his breath; the miracle was an obvious misfire.

It was in the hall the next morning after a late breakfast that Clovis had his final inspiration as he stood engaged in coaxing rust spots from an old putter.

'Where is Miss Martlet?' he asked the butler, who was at that moment crossing the hall.

'Writing letters in the morning-room, sir,' said Sturridge, announcing a fact of which his questioner was already aware.

'She wants to copy the inscription on that old basket-hilted sabre,' said Clovis, pointing to a venerable weapon hanging on the wall. 'I wish you'd take it to her; my hands are all over oil. Take it without the sheath, it will be less trouble.'

The butler drew the blade, still keen and bright in its well-cared-for old age, and carried it into the morning-room. There was a door near the writing-table leading to a back stairway; Jane vanished through it with such lightning rapidity that the butler doubted whether she had seen him come in. Half an hour later Clovis was driving her and her hastily packed luggage to the station.

'Mother will be awfully vexed when she comes back from her ride and finds you have gone,' he observed to the departing guest, 'but I'll make up some story about an urgent wire having called you away. It wouldn't do to alarm her unnecessarily about Sturridge.'

Jane sniffed slightly at Clovis' ideas of unnecessary alarm, and was almost rude to the young man who came round with thoughtful inquiries as to luncheon-baskets.

The miracle lost some of its usefulness from the fact that Dora wrote the same day postponing the date of her visit, but, at any rate, Clovis holds the record as the only human being who ever hustled Jane Martlet out of the time-table of her migrations.

# The Schartz–Metterklume Method

Lady Carlotta stepped out on to the platform of the small wayside station and took a turn or two up and down its uninteresting length, to kill time till the train should be pleased to proceed on its way. Then, in the roadway beyond, she saw a horse struggling with a more than ample load, and a carter of the sort that seems to bear a sullen hatred against the animal that helps him to earn a living. Lady Carlotta promptly betook her to the roadway, and put rather a different complexion on the struggle. Certain of her acquaintances were wont to give her plentiful admonition as to the undesirability of interfering on behalf of a distressed animal, such interference being 'none of her business'. Only once had she put the doctrine of non-interference into practice, when one of its most eloquent exponents had been besieged for nearly three hours in a small and extremely uncomfortable may-tree by an angry boar-pig, while Lady Carlotta, on the other side of the fence, had proceeded with the water-colour sketch she was engaged on, and refused to interfere between the boar and his prisoner. It is to be feared that she lost the friendship of the ultimately rescued lady. On this occasion she merely lost the train, which gave way to the first sign of impatience it had shown throughout the journey, and steamed off without her. She bore the desertion with philosophical indifference; her friends and relations were thoroughly well used to the fact of her luggage arriving without her. She wired a vague noncommittal message to her destination to say that she was coming on 'by another train'. Before she had time to think what her next move might be she was confronted by an imposingly attired lady, who seemed to be taking a prolonged mental inventory of her clothes and looks.

'You must be Miss Hope, the governess I've come to meet,' said the apparition, in a tone that admitted of very little argument.

'Very well, if I must I must,' said Lady Carlotta to herself with dangerous meekness.

'I am Mrs Quabarl,' continued the lady; 'and where, pray, is your luggage?'

'It's gone astray,' said the alleged governess, falling in with the excellent rule of life that the absent are always to blame; the luggage had, in point of fact, behaved with perfect correctitude. 'I've just telegraphed about it,' she added, with a nearer approach to truth.

'How provoking,' said Mrs Quabarl; 'these railway companies are so careless. However, my maid can lend you things for the night,' and she led the way to her car.

During the drive to the Quabarl mansion Lady Carlotta was impressively introduced to the nature of the charge that had been thrust upon her; she learned that Claude and Wilfrid were delicate, sensitive young people, that Irene had the artistic temperament highly developed, and that Viola was something or other else of a mould equally commonplace among children of that class and type in the twentieth century.

'I wish them not only to be *taught*,' said Mrs Quabarl, 'but *interested* in what they learn. In their history lessons, for instance, you must try to make them feel that they are being introduced to the life-stories of men and women who really lived, not merely committing a mass of names and dates to memory. French, of course, I shall expect you to talk at mealtimes several days in the week.'

'I shall talk French four days of the week and Russian in the remaining three.'

'Russian? My dear Miss Hope, no one in the house speaks or understands Russian.'

'That will not embarrass me in the least,' said Lady Carlotta coldly.

Mrs Quabarl, to use a colloquial expression, was knocked off her perch. She was one of those imperfectly self-assured individuals who are magnificent and autocratic as long as they are not seriously opposed. The least show of unexpected resistance goes a long way towards rendering them cowed and apologetic. When the new governess failed to express wondering admiration of the large newly purchased and expensive car, and lightly alluded to the superior advantages of one or two makes which had just been put on the market, the discomfiture of her patroness became almost abject. Her feelings were those which might have animated a general of ancient warfaring days, on beholding his heaviest battle-elephant ignominiously driven off the field by slingers and javelin throwers.

At dinner that evening, although reinforced by her husband, who usually duplicated her opinions and lent her moral support generally, Mrs Quabarl regained none of her lost ground. The governess not only helped herself well and truly to wine, but held forth with considerable show of critical knowledge on various vintage matters, concerning which the Quabarls were in no wise able to pose as authorities. Previous governesses had limited their conversation on the wine topic to a respectful and doubtless sincere expression of a preference for water. When this one went as far as to recommend a wine firm in whose hands you could not go very far wrong Mrs Quabarl thought it time to turn the conversation into more usual channels.

'We got very satisfactory references about you from Canon Teep,' she observed; 'a very estimable man, I should think.'

'Drinks like a fish and beats his wife, otherwise a very lovable character,' said the governess imperturbably.

'My *dear* Miss Hope! I trust you are exaggerating,' exclaimed the Quabarls in unison.

'One must in justice admit that there is some provocation,' continued the romancer. 'Mrs Teep is quite the most irritating bridge-player that I have ever sat down with; her leads and declarations would condone a certain amount of brutality in her partner, but to souse her with the contents of the only soda-water syphon in the house on a Sunday afternoon, when one couldn't get another, argues an indifference to the comfort of others which I cannot altogether overlook. You may think me hasty in my judgments, but it was practically on account of the syphon incident that I left.'

'We will talk of this some other time,' said Mrs Quabarl hastily.

'I shall never allude to it again,' said the governess with decision.

Mr Quabarl made a welcome diversion by asking what studies the new instructress proposed to inaugurate on the morrow.

'History to begin with,' she informed him.

'Ah, history,' he observed sagely; 'now in teaching them history you must take care to interest them in what they learn. You must make them feel that they are being introduced to the life-stories of men and women who really lived –'

'I've told her all that,' interposed Mrs Quabarl.

'I teach history on the Schartz–Metterklume method,' said the governess loftily.

'Ah, yes,' said her listeners, thinking it expedient to assume an acquaintance at least with the name.

'What are you children doing out here?' demanded Mrs Quabarl the next morning, on finding Irene sitting rather glumly at the head of the stairs, while her sister was perched in an attitude of depressed discomfort on the window-seat behind her, with a wolf-skin rug almost covering her.

'We are having a history lesson,' came the unexpected reply. 'I am supposed to be Rome, and Viola up there is the she-wolf; not a real wolf, but the figure of one that the Romans used to set store by – I forget why. Claude and Wilfrid have gone to fetch the shabby women.'

'The shabby women?'

'Yes, they've got to carry them off. They didn't want to, but Miss Hope got one of father's fives-bats and said she'd give them a number-nine spanking if they didn't, so they've gone to do it.'

A loud, angry screaming from the direction of the lawn drew Mrs Quabarl thither in hot haste, fearful lest the threatened castigation might even now be in process of infliction. The outcry, however, came principally from the two small daughters of the lodge-keeper, who were being hauled and pushed towards the house by the panting and dishevelled Claude and Wilfrid, whose task was rendered even more arduous by the incessant, if not very effectual, attacks of the captured maidens' small brother. The governess, fives-bat in hand, sat negligently on the stone balustrade, presiding over the scene with the cold impartiality of a Goddess of Battles. A furious and repeated chorus of 'I'll tell muvver' rose from the lodge children, but the lodge-mother, who was hard of hearing, was for the moment immersed in the preoccupation of her washtub. After an apprehensive glance in the direction of the lodge (the good woman was gifted with the highly militant temper which is sometimes the privilege of 63 deafness) Mrs Quabarl flew indignantly to the rescue of the struggling captives.

'Wilfrid! Claude! Let those children go at once. Miss Hope, what on earth is the meaning of this scene?'

'Early Roman history; the Sabine women, don't you know? It's the Schartz–Metterklume method to make children understand history by acting it themselves; fixes it in their memory, you know. Of course, if, thanks to your interference, your boys go through life thinking that the Sabine women ultimately escaped, I really cannot be held responsible.'

'You may be very clever and modern, Miss Hope,' said Mrs Quabarl firmly, 'but I should like you to leave here by the next train. Your luggage will be sent after you as soon as it arrives.'

'I'm not certain exactly where I shall be for the next few days,' said the dismissed instructress of youth; 'you might keep my luggage till I wire my address. There are only a couple of trunks and some golf-clubs and a leopard cub.'

'A leopard cub!' gasped Mrs Quabarl. Even in her departure this extraordinary person seemed destined to leave a trail of embarrassment behind her.

'Well, it's rather left off being a cub; it's more than half-grown, you know. A fowl every day and a rabbit on Sundays is what it usually gets. Raw beef makes it too excitable. Don't trouble about getting the car for me, I'm rather inclined for a walk.'

And Lady Carlotta strode out of the Quabarl horizon.

The advent of the genuine Miss Hope, who had made a mistake as to the day on which she was due to arrive, caused a turmoil which that good lady was quite unused to inspiring. Obviously the Quabarl family had been woefully befooled, but a certain amount of relief came with the knowledge.

'How tiresome for you, dear Carlotta,' said her hostess, when the overdue guest ultimately arrived; 'how very tiresome losing your train and having to stop overnight in a strange place.'

'Oh, dear no,' said Lady Carlotta; 'not at all tiresome – for me.'

'It's not the daily grind that I complain of,' said Blenkinthrope resentfully; 'it's the dull grey sameness of my life outside of office hours. Nothing of interest comes my way, nothing remarkable or out of the common. Even the little things that I do try to find some interest in don't seem to interest other people. Things in my garden, for instance.'

'The potato that weighed just over two pounds,' said his friend Gorworth.

'Did I tell you about that?' said Blenkinthrope; 'I was telling the others in the train this morning. I forgot if I'd told you.'

'To be exact you told me that it weighed just under two pounds, but I took into account the fact that abnormal vegetables and fresh-water fish have an after-life, in which growth is not arrested.'

'You're just like the others,' said Blenkinthrope sadly, 'you only make fun of it.'

'The fault is with the potato, not with us,' said Gorworth; 'we are not in the least interested in it because it is not in the least interesting. The men you go up in the train with every day are just in the same case as yourself; their lives are commonplace and not very interesting to themselves, and they certainly are not going to wax enthusiastic over the commonplace events in other men's lives. Tell them something startling, dramatic, piquant, that has happened to yourself or to some one in your family, and you will capture their interest at once. They will talk about you with a certain personal pride to all their acquaintances. "Man I know intimately, fellow called Blenkinthrope, lives down my way, had two of his fingers clawed clean off by a lobster he was carrying home to supper. Doctor says entire hand may have to come off." Now that is conversation of a very high order. But imagine walking into a tennis club with the remark: "I know a man who has grown a potato weighing two and a quarter pounds."'

'But hang it all, my dear fellow,' said Blenkinthrope impatiently, 'haven't I just told you that nothing of a remarkable nature ever happens to me?'

'Invent something,' said Gorworth. Since winning a prize for excellence in scriptural knowledge at a preparatory school he had felt licensed to be a little more unscrupulous than the circle he moved in. Much might surely be excused to one who in early life could give a list of seventeen trees mentioned in the Old Testament.

'What sort of thing?' asked Blenkinthrope, somewhat snappishly.

'A snake got into your hen-run yesterday morning and killed six out of seven pullets, first mesmerizing them with its eyes and then biting them as they stood helpless. The seventh pullet was one of that French sort, with feathers all over its eyes, so it escaped the mesmeric snare, and just flew at what it could see of the snake and pecked it to pieces.'

'Thank you,' said Blenkinthrope stiffly; 'it's a very clever invention. If such a thing had really happened in my poultry-run I admit I should have been proud and interested to tell people about it. But I'd rather stick to fact, even if it is plain fact.' All the same his mind dwelt wistfully on the story of the Seventh Pullet. He could picture himself telling it in the train amid the absorbed interest of his fellow-passengers. Unconsciously all sorts of little details and improvements began to suggest themselves.

Wistfulness was still his dominant mood when he took his seat in the railway carriage the next morning. Opposite him sat Stevenham, who had attained to a recognized brevet of importance through the fact of an uncle having dropped dead in the act of voting at a parliamentary election. That had happened three years ago, but Stevenham was still deferred to on all questions of home and foreign politics.

'Hullo, how's the giant mushroom, or whatever it was?' was all the notice Blenkinthrope got from his fellow travellers.

Young Duckby, whom he mildly disliked, speedily monopolized the general attention by an account of a domestic bereavement.

'Had four young pigeons carried off last night by a whacking big rat. Oh, a monster he must have been; you could tell by the size of the hole he made breaking into the loft.'

No moderate-sized rat ever seemed to carry out any predatory operations in these regions; they were all enormous in their enormity.

'Pretty hard lines that,' continued Duckby, seeing that he had secured the attention and respect of the company; 'four squeakers carried off at one swoop. You'd find it rather hard to match that in the way of unlooked-for bad luck.'

'I had six pullets out of a pen of seven killed by a snake yesterday afternoon,' said Blenkinthrope, in a voice which he hardly recognized as his own.

'By a snake?' came in excited chorus.

'It fascinated them with its deadly, glittering eyes, one after the other, and struck them down while they stood helpless. A bedridden neighbour, who wasn't able to call for assistance, witnessed it all from her bedroom window.'

68

'Well, I never!' broke in the chorus, with variations.

'The interesting part of it is about the seventh pullet, the one that didn't get killed,' resumed Blenkinthrope, slowly lighting a cigarette. His diffidence had left him, and he was beginning to realize how safe and easy depravity can seem once one has the courage to begin. 'The six dead birds were Minorcas; the seventh was a Houdan with a mop of feathers all over its eyes. It could hardly see the snake at all, so of course it wasn't mesmerized like the others. It just could see something wriggling on the ground, and went for it and pecked it to death.'

'Well, I'm blessed!' exclaimed the chorus.

In the course of the next few days Blenkinthrope discovered how little the loss of one's self-respect affects one who has gained the esteem of the world. His story found its way into one of the poultry papers, and was copied thence into a daily news-sheet as a matter of general interest. A lady wrote from the North of Scotland recounting a similar episode which she had witnessed as occurring between a stoat and a blind grouse. Somehow a lie seems so much less reprehensible when one can call it a lee.

For a while the adapter of the Seventh Pullet story enjoyed to the full his altered standing as a person of consequence, one who had had some share in the strange events of his times. Then he was thrust once again into the cold grey background by the sudden blossoming into importance of Smith-Paddon, a daily fellow-traveller, whose little girl had been knocked down and nearly hurt by a car belonging to a musical-comedy actress. The actress was not in the car at the time, but she was in numerous photographs which appeared in the illustrated papers of Zoto Dobreen inquiring after the well-being of Maisie, daughter of Edmund Smith-Paddon, Esq. With this new human interest to

69

absorb them the travelling companions were almost rude when Blenkinthrope tried to explain his contrivance for keeping vipers and peregrine falcons out of his chicken-run.

Gorworth, to whom he unburdened himself in private, gave him the same counsel as theretofore.

'Invent something.'

'Yes, but what?'

The ready affirmative coupled with the question betrayed a significant shifting of the ethical standpoint.

It was a few days later that Blenkinthrope revealed a chapter of family history to the customary gathering in the railway carriage.

'Curious thing happened to my aunt, the one who lives in Paris,' he began. He had several aunts, but they were all geographically distributed over Greater London.

'She was sitting on a seat in the Bois the other afternoon, after lunching at the Roumanian Legation.'

Whatever the story gained in picturesqueness for the dragging-in of diplomatic 'atmosphere', it ceased from that moment to command any acceptance as a record of current events. Gorworth had warned his neophyte that this would be the case, but the traditional enthusiasm of the neophyte had triumphed over discretion.

'She was feeling rather drowsy, the effect probably of the Champagne, which she's not in the habit of taking in the middle of the day.'

A subdued murmur of admiration went round the company. Blenkinthrope's aunts were not used to taking Champagne in the middle of the year, regarding it exclusively as a Christmas and New Year accessory.

'Presently a rather portly gentleman passed by her seat and

paused an instant to light a cigar. At that moment a youngish man came up behind him, drew the blade from a swordstick, and stabbed him half a dozen times through and through. "Scoundrel," he cried to his victim, "you do not know me. My name is Henri Leturc." The elder man wiped away some of the blood that was spattering his clothes, turned to his assailant, and said: "And since when has an attempted assassination been considered an introduction?" Then he finished lighting his cigar and walked away. My aunt had intended screaming for the police, but seeing the indifference with which the principal in the affair had treated the matter she felt that it would be an impertinence on her part to interfere. Of course I need hardly say she put the whole thing down to the effects of a warm, drowsy afternoon and the Legation Champagne. Now comes the astonishing part of my story. A fortnight later a bank manager was stabbed to death with a swordstick in that very part of the Bois. His assassin was the son of a charwoman formerly working at the bank, who had been dismissed from her job by the manager on account of chronic intemperance. His name was Henri Leturc.'

From that moment Blenkinthrope was tacitly accepted as the Munchausen of the party. No effort was spared to draw him out from day to day in the exercise of testing their powers of credulity, and Blenkinthrope, in the false security of an assured and receptive audience, waxed industrious and ingenious in supplying the demand for marvels. Duckby's satirical story of a tame otter that had a tank in the garden to swim in, and whined restlessly whenever the water-rate was overdue, was scarcely an unfair parody of some of Blenkinthrope's wilder efforts. And then one day came Nemesis.

Returning to his villa one evening Blenkinthrope found his wife sitting in front of a pack of cards, which she was scrutinizing with unusual concentration.

71

'The same old patience-game?' he asked carelessly.

'No, dear; this is the Death's Head patience, the most difficult of them all. I've never got it to work out, and somehow I should be rather frightened if I did. Mother only got it out once in her life; she was afraid of it, too. Her great-aunt had done it once and fallen dead from excitement the next moment, and mother always had a feeling that she would die if she ever got it out. She died the same night that she did it. She was in bad health at the time, certainly, but it was a strange coincidence.'

'Don't do it if it frightens you,' was Blenkinthrope's practical comment as he left the room. A few minutes later his wife called to him.

'John, it gave me such a turn, I nearly got it out. Only the five of diamonds held me up at the end. I really thought I'd done it.'

'Why, you can do it,' said Blenkinthrope, who had come back to the room; 'if you shift the eight of clubs on to that open nine the five can be moved on to the six.'

His wife made the suggested move with hasty, trembling fingers, and piled the outstanding cards on their respective packs. Then she followed the example of her mother and great-grand-aunt.

Blenkinthrope had been genuinely fond of his wife, but in the midst of his bereavement one dominant thought obtruded itself. Something sensational and real had at last come into his life; no longer was it a grey, colourless record. The headlines which might appropriately describe his domestic tragedy kept shaping themselves in his brain. 'Inherited presentiment comes true'. 'The Death's Head patience: Card-game that justified its sinister name in three generations'. He wrote out the full story of the fatal occurrence for the *Essex Vedette*, the editor of which was a friend of his, and to another friend he gave a condensed account, to be taken up to the office of the halfpenny dailies. But in both cases his reputation as a romancer stood fatally in the way of the fulfilment of his ambitions. 'Not the right thing to be Munchausening in a time of sorrow,' agreed his friends among themselves, and a brief note of regret at the 'sudden death of the wife of our respected neighbour, Mr John Blenkinthrope, from heart failure', appearing in the news column of the local paper was the forlorn outcome of his visions of widespread publicity.

Blenkinthrope shrank from the society of his erstwhile travelling companions and took to travelling townwards by an earlier train. He sometimes tries to enlist the sympathy and attention of a chance acquaintance in details of the whistling prowess of his best canary or the dimensions of his largest beetroot; he scarcely recognizes himself as the man who was once spoken about and pointed out as the owner of the Seventh Pullet.

# The Forbidden Buzzards

'Is matchmaking at all in your line?'

Hugo Peterby asked the question with a certain amount of personal interest.

'I don't specialize in it,' said Clovis; 'it's all right while you're doing it, but the after-effects are sometimes so disconcerting – the mute reproachful looks of the people you've aided and abetted in matrimonial experiments. It's as bad as selling a man a horse with half a dozen latent vices and watching him discover them piecemeal in the course of the hunting season. I suppose you're thinking of the Coulterneb girl. She's certainly jolly, and quite all right as far as looks go, and I believe a certain amount of money adheres to her. What I don't see is how you will ever manage to propose to her. In all the time I've known her I don't remember her to have stopped talking for three consecutive minutes. You'll have to race her six times round the grass paddock for a bet, and then blurt your proposal out before she's got her wind back. The paddock is laid up for hay, but if you're really in love with her you won't let a consideration of that sort stop you, especially as it's not your hay.'

'I think I could manage the proposing part right enough,' said Hugo, 'if I could count on being left alone with her for four or five hours. The trouble is that I'm not likely to get anything like that amount of grace. That fellow Lanner is showing signs of interesting himself in the same quarter. He's quite heartbreakingly rich and is rather a swell in his way; in fact, our hostess is obviously a bit flattered at having him here. If she gets wind of the fact that he's inclined to be attracted by Betty Coulterneb she'll think it a splendid match and throw them into each other's arms all day long, and then where will my opportunities come in? My one anxiety is to keep him out of the girl's way as much as possible, and if you could help me –'

'If you want me to trot Lanner round the countryside, inspecting alleged Roman remains and studying local methods of bee culture and crop raising, I'm afraid I can't oblige you,' said Clovis. 'You see, he's taken something of an aversion to me since the other night in the smoking-room.'

'What happened in the smoking-room?'

'He trotted out some well-worn chestnut as the latest thing in good stories, and I remarked, quite innocently, that I never could remember whether it was George II or James II who was so fond of that particular story, and now he regards me with politely draped dislike. I'll do my best for you, if the opportunity arises, but it will have to be in a roundabout, impersonal manner.'

'It's so nice having Mr Lanner here,' confided Mrs Olston to Clovis the next afternoon; 'he's always been engaged when I've asked him before. Such a nice man; he really ought to be married to some nice girl. Between you and me, I have an idea that he came down here for a certain reason.'

'I've had much the same idea,' said Clovis, lowering his voice; 'in fact, I'm almost certain of it.'

'You mean he's attracted by –' began Mrs Olston eagerly.

'I mean he's here for what he can get,' said Clovis.

'For what he can *get*?' said the hostess with a touch of indignation in her voice; 'What do you mean? He's a very rich man. What should he want to get here?'

'He has one ruling passion,' said Clovis, 'and there's something he can get here that is not to be had for love nor for money anywhere else in the country, as far as I know.'

'But what? Whatever do you mean? What is his ruling passion?'

'Egg-collecting,' said Clovis. 'He has agents all over the world getting rare eggs for him, and his collection is one of the finest in Europe; but his great ambition is to collect his treasures personally. He stops at no expense nor trouble to achieve that end.'

'Good heavens! The buzzards, the rough-legged buzzards!' exclaimed Mrs Olston; 'you don't think he's going to raid their nest?'

'What do you think yourself?' asked Clovis; 'the only pair of rough-legged buzzards known to breed in this country are nesting in your woods. Very few people know about them, but as a member of the league for protecting rare birds that information would be at his disposal. I came down in the train with him, and I noticed that a bulky volume of Dresser's *Birds of Europe* was one of the requisites that he had packed in his travelling-kit. It was the volume dealing with short-winged hawks and buzzards.'

Clovis believed that if a lie was worth telling it was worth telling well.

'This is appalling,' said Mrs Olston; 'my husband would never forgive me if anything happened to those birds. They've been seen about the woods for the last year or two, but this is the first time they've nested. As you say, they are almost the only pair known to be breeding in the whole of Great Britain; and now their nest is going to be harried by a guest staying under my roof. I must do something to stop it. Do you think if I appealed to him –?'

Clovis laughed.

'There is a story going about, which I fancy is true in most of its details, of something that happened not long ago somewhere on the coast of the Sea of Marmora, in which our friend had a hand. A Syrian nightjar, or some such bird, was known to be breeding in the olive gardens of a rich Armenian, who for some reason or other wouldn't allow Lanner to go in and take the eggs though he offered cash down for the permission. The Armenian was found beaten near to death a day or two later, and his fences levelled. It was assumed to be a case of Mussulman aggression, and noted as such in all the Consular reports, but the eggs are in the Lanner collection. No, I don't think I should appeal to his better feelings if I were you.'

'I must do something,' said Mrs Olston tearfully; 'my husband's parting words when he went off to Norway were an injunction to see that those birds were not disturbed, and he's asked about them every time he's written. Do suggest something.'

'I was going to suggest picketing,' said Clovis.

'Picketing! You mean setting guards round the birds?'

'No; round Lanner. He can't find his way through those woods by night, and you could arrange that you or Evelyn or Jack or the German governess should be by his side in relays all day long. A fellow guest he could get rid of, but he couldn't very well shake off members of the household, and even the most determined collector would hardly go climbing after forbidden buzzards' eggs with a German governess hanging round his neck, so to speak.'

Lanner, who had been lazily watching for an opportunity for prosecuting his courtship of the Coulterneb girl, found presently that his chances of getting her to himself for ten minutes even were nonexistent. If the girl was ever alone he never was. His 77 hostess had changed suddenly, as far as he was concerned, from the desirable type that lets her guests do nothing in the way that best pleases them, to the sort that drags them over the ground like so many harrows. She showed him the herb garden and the greenhouses, the village church, some water-colour sketches that her sister had done in Corsica, and the place where it was hoped that celery would grow later in the year. He was shown all the Aylesbury ducklings and the row of wooden hives where there would have been bees if there had not been bee disease. He was also taken to the end of a long lane and shown a distant mound whereon local tradition reported that the Danes had once pitched a camp. And when his hostess had to desert him temporarily for other duties he would find Evelyn walking solemnly by his side. Evelyn was fourteen and talked chiefly about good and evil, and of how much one might accomplish in the way of regenerating the world if one was thoroughly determined to do one's utmost. It was generally rather a relief when she was displaced by Jack, who was nine years old, and talked exclusively about the Balkan War without throwing any fresh light on its political or military history. The German governess told Lanner more about Schiller than he had ever heard in his life about any one person; it was perhaps his own fault for having told her that he was not interested in Goethe. When the governess went off picket duty the hostess was again on hand with a not-to-be-gainsaid invitation to visit the cottage of an old woman who remembered Charles James Fox; the woman had been dead for two or three years, but the cottage was still there. Lanner was called back to town earlier than he had originally intended.

Hugo did not bring off his affair with Betty Coulterneb. Whether she refused him or whether, as was more generally supposed, he did not get a chance of saying three consecutive words, has never been exactly ascertained. Anyhow, she is still the jolly Coulterneb girl.

The buzzards successfully reared two young ones, which were shot by a local hairdresser.

# A Holiday Task

Kenelm Jerton entered the dining-hall of the Golden Galleon Hotel in the full crush of the luncheon hour. Nearly every seat was occupied, and small additional tables had been brought in, where floor space permitted, to accommodate late-comers, with the result that many of the tables were almost touching each other. Jerton was beckoned by a waiter to the only vacant table that was discernible, and took his seat with the uncomfortable and wholly groundless idea that every one in the room was staring at him. He was a youngish man of ordinary appearance, quiet of dress and unobtrusive of manner, and he could never wholly rid himself of the idea that a fierce light of public scrutiny beat on' him as though he had been a notability or a super-nut. After he had ordered his lunch there came the unavoidable interval of waiting, with nothing to do but to stare at the flower-vase on his table and to be stared at (in imagination) by several flappers, some maturer beings of the same sex, and a satirical-looking Jew. In order to carry off the situation with some appearance of unconcern he became spuriously interested in the contents of the flower-vase.

'What is the name of these roses, d'you know?' he asked the waiter. The waiter was ready at all times to conceal his ignorance concerning items of the wine-list or *menu*; he was frankly ignorant as to the specific name of the roses.

'*Amy Silvester Partington*,' said a voice at Jerton's elbow.

The voice came from a pleasant-faced, well-dressed young woman who was sitting at a table that almost touched Jerton's.

He thanked her hurriedly and nervously for the information, and made some inconsequent remark about the flowers.

'It is a curious thing,' said the young woman, 'that I should be able to tell you the name of those roses without an effort of memory, because if you were to ask me my name I should be utterly unable to give it to you.'

Jerton had not harboured the least intention of extending his thirst for name-labels to his neighbour. After her rather remarkable announcement, however, he was obliged to say something in the way of polite inquiry.

'Yes,' answered the lady, 'I suppose it is a case of partial loss of memory. I was in the train coming down here; my ticket told me that I had come from Victoria and was bound for this place. I had a couple of five-pound notes and a sovereign on me, no visiting cards or any other means of identification, and no idea as to who I am. I can only hazily recollect that I have a title; I am Lady Somebody – beyond that my mind is a blank.'

'Hadn't you any luggage with you?' asked Jerton.

'That is what I didn't know. I knew the name of this hotel and made up my mind to come here, and when the hotel porter who meets the trains asked if I had any luggage I had to invent a dressing-bag and dress-basket; I could always pretend that they had gone astray. I gave him the name of Smith, and presently he emerged from a confused pile of luggage and passengers with a dressing-bag and dress-basket labelled Kestrel-Smith. I had to take them; I don't see what else I could have done.'

Jerton said nothing, but he rather wondered what the lawful owner of the baggage would do.

'Of course it was dreadful arriving at a strange hotel with the name of Kestrel-Smith, but it would have been worse to have arrived without luggage. Anyhow, I hate causing trouble.'

Jerton had visions of harassed railway officials and distraught Kestrel-Smiths, but he made no attempt to clothe his mental picture in words. The lady continued her story.

'Naturally, none of my keys would fit the things, but I told an intelligent page boy that I had lost my key-ring, and he had the locks forced in a twinkling. Rather too intelligent, that boy; he will probably end in Dartmoor. The Kestrel-Smith toilet tools aren't up to much, but they are better than nothing.'

'If you feel sure that you have a title,' said Jerton, 'why not get hold of a peerage and go right through it?'

'I tried that. I skimmed through the list of the House of Lords in *Whitaker*, but a mere printed string of names conveys awfully little to one, you know. If you were an army officer and had lost your identity you might pore over the Army List for months without finding out who you were. I'm going on another tack; I'm trying to find out by various little tests who I am *not* – that will narrow the range of uncertainty down a bit. You may have noticed, for instance, that I'm lunching principally off lobster Newburg.'

Jerton had not ventured to notice anything of the sort.

'It's an extravagance, because it's one of the most expensive dishes on the menu, but at any rate it proves that I'm not Lady Starping; she never touches shell-fish, and poor Lady Braddleshrub has no digestion at all; if I am *her* I shall certainly die in agony in the course of the afternoon, and the duty of finding out who I am will devolve on the press and the police and those sort of people; I shall be past caring. Lady Knewford doesn't know one rose from another and she hates men, so she wouldn't have spoken to you in any case; and Lady Mousehilton flirts with every man she meets – I haven't flirted with you, have I?'

Jerton hastily gave the required assurance.

'Well, you see,' continued the lady, 'that knocks four off the list at once.'

'It'll be rather a lengthy process bringing the list down to one,' said Jerton.

'Oh, but, of course, there are heaps of them that I couldn't possibly be – women who've got grandchildren or sons old enough to have celebrated their coming of age. I've only got to consider the ones about my own age. I tell you how you might help me this afternoon, if you don't mind; go through any of the back numbers of *Country Life* and those sort of papers that you can find in the smoking-room, and see if you come across my portrait with infant son or anything of that sort. It won't take you ten minutes. I'll meet you in the lounge about tea-time. Thanks awfully.'

And the Fair Unknown, having graciously pressed Jerton into the search for her lost identity, rose and left the room. As she passed the young man's table she halted for a moment and whispered:

'Did you notice that I tipped the waiter a shilling? We can cross Lady Ulwight off the list; she would have died rather than do that.'

At five o'clock Jerton made his way to the hotel lounge; he had spent a diligent but fruitless quarter of an hour among the illustrated weeklies in the smoking-room. His new acquaintance was seated at a small tea-table, with a waiter hovering in attendance.

'China tea or Indian?' she asked as Jerton came up.

'China, please, and nothing to eat. Have you discovered anything?'

'Only negative information. I'm not Lady Befnal. She disapproves dreadfully at any form of gambling, so when I recognized 83 a well-known book-maker in the hotel lobby I went and put a tenner on an unnamed filly by William the Third out of Mitrovitza for the three-fifteen race. I suppose the fact of the animal being nameless was what attracted me.'

'Did it win?' asked Jerton.

'No, came in fourth, the most irritating thing a horse can do when you've backed it win or place. Anyhow, I know now that I'm not Lady Befnal.'

'It seems to me that the knowledge was rather dearly bought,' commented Jerton.

'Well, yes, it has rather cleared me out,' admitted the identity-seeker; 'a florin is about all I've got left on me. The lobster Newburg made my lunch rather an expensive one, and, of course, I had to tip that boy for what he did to the Kestrel-Smith locks. I've got rather a useful idea, though. I feel certain that I belong to the Pivot Club; I'll go back to town and ask the hall porter there if there are any letters for me. He knows all the members by sight, and if there are any letters or telephone messages waiting for me, of course that will solve the problem. If he says there aren't any, I shall say: "You know who I am, don't you?" so I'll find out anyway.'

The plan seemed a sound one; a difficulty in its execution suggested itself to Jerton.

'Of course,' said the lady, when he hinted at the obstacle, 'there's my fare back to town, and my bill here and cabs and things. If you lend me three pounds that ought to see me through comfortably. Thanks ever so. Then there is the question of that luggage: I don't want to be saddled with that for the rest of my life. I'll have it brought down to the hall and you can pretend to mount guard over it while I'm writing a letter. Then I shall just slip away to the station, and you can wander off to the smoking-room, and they can do what they like with the things. They'll advertise them after a bit and the owner can claim them.'

Jerton acquiesced in the manoeuvre, and duly mounted guard over the luggage while its temporary owner slipped unobtrusively out of the hotel. Her departure was not, however, altogether unnoticed. Two gentlemen were strolling past Jerton, and one of them remarked to the other:

'Did you see that tall woman in grey who went out just now? She is the Lady –'

His promenade carried him out of earshot at the critical moment when he was about to disclose the elusive identity. The Lady Who? Jerton could scarcely run after a total stranger, break into his conversation, and ask him for information concerning a chance passer-by. Besides, it was desirable that he should keep up the appearance of looking after the luggage. In a minute or two, however, the important personage, the man who knew, came strolling back alone. Jerton summoned up all his courage and waylaid him.

'I think I heard you say you knew the lady who went out of the hotel a few minutes ago, a tall lady, dressed in grey. Excuse me for asking if you could tell me her name; I've been talking to her for half an hour; she – er – she knows all my people and seems to know me, so I suppose I've met her somewhere before, but I'm blest if I can put a name to her. Could you –?'

'Certainly. She's a Mrs Stroope.'

'*Mrs*?' queried Jerton.

'Yes, she's the Lady Champion at golf in my part of the world. An awful good sort, and goes about a good deal in Society, but she has an awkward habit of losing her memory every now and then, and get into all sorts of fixes. She's furious, too, if you make any allusion to it afterwards. Good day, sir.'

The stranger passed on his way, and before Jerton had had time to assimilate his information he found his whole attention centred on an angry-looking lady who was making loud and fretful-seeming inquiries of the hotel clerks.

'Has any luggage been brought here from the station by mistake, a dress-basket and dressing-case, with the name Kestrel-Smith? It can't be traced anywhere. I saw it put in at Victoria, that I'll swear. Why – there *is* my luggage! and the locks have been tampered with!'

Jerton heard no more. He fled down to the Turkish bath, and stayed there for hours.

# PENGUIN 60s

MARTIN AMIS · *God's Dice*
HANS CHRISTIAN ANDERSEN · *The Emperor's New Clothes*
MARCUS AURELIUS · *Meditations*
JAMES BALDWIN · *Sonny's Blues*
AMBROSE BIERCE · *An Occurrence at Owl Creek Bridge*
DIRK BOGARDE · *From Le Pigeonnier*
WILLIAM BOYD · *Killing Lizards*
POPPY Z. BRITE · *His Mouth will Taste of Wormwood*
ITALO CALVINO · *Ten Italian Folktales*
ALBERT CAMUS · *Summer*
TRUMAN CAPOTE · *First and Last*
RAYMOND CHANDLER · *Goldfish*
ANTON CHEKHOV · *The Black Monk*
ROALD DAHL · *Lamb to the Slaughter*
ELIZABETH DAVID · *I'll be with You in the Squeezing of a Lemon*
N. J. DAWOOD (TRANS.) · *The Seven Voyages of Sindbad the Sailor*
ISAK DINESEN · *The Dreaming Child*
SIR ARTHUR CONAN DOYLE · *The Man with the Twisted Lip*
DICK FRANCIS · *Racing Classics*
SIGMUND FREUD · *Five Lectures on Psycho-Analysis*
KAHLIL GIBRAN · *Prophet, Madman, Wanderer*
STEPHEN JAY GOULD · *Adam's Navel*
ALASDAIR GRAY · *Five Letters from an Eastern Empire*
GRAHAM GREENE · *Under the Garden*
JAMES HERRIOT · *Seven Yorkshire Tales*
PATRICIA HIGHSMITH · *Little Tales of Misogyny*
M. R. JAMES AND R. L. STEVENSON · *The Haunted Dolls' House*
RUDYARD KIPLING · *Baa Baa, Black Sheep*
PENELOPE LIVELY · *A Long Night at Abu Simbel*
KATHERINE MANSFIELD · *The Escape*

# PENGUIN 60s

GABRIEL GARCÍA MÁRQUEZ · *Bon Voyage, Mr President*
PATRICK MCGRATH · *The Angel*
HERMAN MELVILLE · *Bartleby*
SPIKE MILLIGAN · *Gunner Milligan, 954024*
MICHEL DE MONTAIGNE · *Four Essays*
JAN MORRIS · *From the Four Corners*
JOHN MORTIMER · *Rumpole and the Younger Generation*
R. K. NARAYAN · *Tales from Malgudi*
ANAÏS NIN · *A Model*
FRANK O'CONNOR · *The Genius*
GEORGE ORWELL · *Pages from a Scullion's Diary*
CAMILLE PAGLIA · *Sex and Violence, or Nature and Art*
SARA PARETSKY · *A Taste of Life*
EDGAR ALLAN POE · *The Pit and the Pendulum*
MISS READ · *Village Christmas*
JEAN RHYS · *Let Them Call It Jazz*
DAMON RUNYON · *The Snatching of Bookie Bob*
SAKI · *The Secret Sin of Septimus Brope*
WILL SELF · *Scale*
GEORGES SIMENON · *Death of a Nobody*
MURIEL SPARK · *The Portobello Road*
ROBERT LOUIS STEVENSON · *The Pavilion on the Links*
PAUL THEROUX · *Down the Yangtze*
WILLIAM TREVOR · *Matilda's England*
MARK TULLY · *Ram Chander's Story*
JOHN UPDIKE · *Friends from Philadelphia*
EUDORA WELTY · *Why I Live at the P. O.*
EDITH WHARTON · *Madame de Treymes*
OSCAR WILDE · *The Happy Prince*
VIRGINIA WOOLF · *Killing the Angel in the House*

# READ MORE IN PENGUIN

For complete information about books available from Penguin and how to order them, please write to us at the appropriate address below. Please note that for copyright reasons the selection of books varies from country to country.

IN THE UNITED KINGDOM: Please write to *Dept. JC, Penguin Books Ltd, FREEPOST, West Drayton, Middlesex UB7 0BR.*
If you have any difficulty in obtaining a title, please send your order with the correct money, plus ten per cent for postage and packaging, to *PO Box No. 11, West Drayton, Middlesex UB7 0BR.*

IN THE UNITED STATES: Please write to *Consumer Sales, Penguin USA, P.O. Box 999, Dept. 17109, Bergenfield, New Jersey 07621-0120.* VISA and MasterCard holders call 1-800-253-6476 to order all Penguin titles.

IN CANADA: Please write to *Penguin Books Canada Ltd, 10 Alcorn Avenue, Suite 300, Toronto, Ontario M4V 3B2.*

IN AUSTRALIA: Please write to *Penguin Books Australia Ltd, P.O. Box 257, Ringwood, Victoria 3134.*

IN NEW ZEALAND: Please write to *Penguin Books (NZ) Ltd, Private Bag 102902, North Shore Mail Centre, Auckland 10.*

IN INDIA: Please write to *Penguin Books India Pvt Ltd, 706 Eros Apartments, 56 Nehru Place, New Delhi 110 019.*

IN THE NETHERLANDS: Please write to *Penguin Books Netherlands bv, Postbus 3507, NL-1001 AH Amsterdam.*

IN GERMANY: Please write to *Penguin Books Deutschland GmbH, Metzlerstrasse 26, 60594 Frankfurt am Main.*

IN SPAIN: Please write to *Penguin Books S. A., Bravo Murillo 19, 1o B, 28015 Madrid.*

IN ITALY: Please write to *Penguin Italia s.r.l., Via Felice Casati 20, I-20124 Milano.*

IN FRANCE: Please write to *Penguin France S. A., 17 rue Lejeune, F-31000 Toulouse.*

IN JAPAN: Please write to *Penguin Books Japan, Ishikiribashi Building, 2-5-4, Suido, Bunkyo-ku, Tokyo 112.*

IN GREECE: Please write to *Penguin Hellas Ltd, Dimocritou 3, GR-106 71 Athens.*

IN SOUTH AFRICA: Please write to *Longman Penguin Southern Africa (Pty) Ltd, Private Bag X08, Bertsham 2013.*